Light *upon* Light

Praise for *At the Still Point: A Literary
Guide to Prayer in Ordinary Time*

I may just be a bit smitten with this book.
—Ann Voskamp, author of *One Thousand Gifts*

A thing of beauty!
—Phyllis Tickle, author of *The Divine Hours*
and *The Great Emergence*

What a delight, to find so extraordinary a collection
meant for use in "ordinary time."
—Kathleen Norris, author of *Dakota* and *The Cloister Walk*

A literary treasure store and a devotional feast.
—Leland Ryken, professor emeritus, Wheaton College

Arthur's selections and compositions make the heart sing
and give the mind pause, cause my soul to pray and
my body increasing time for Sabbath.
—Bishop Jonathan D. Keaton, coauthor of
*The Confessions of Three Ebony Bishop*s

A timely and salutary achievement.
—the late Christopher W. Mitchell, professor,
Torrey Honors Institute, Biola University

More than just a net for harvesting the best spiritual moments
in fiction and poetry, *At the Still Point* imparts these readings in
the form of a devotional so that, with daily discipline, they
may cultivate the reverence, wonder and attention necessary
to recognizing Christ in the ordinary.
—*Image* journal review

Light *upon* Light

A Literary Guide to Prayer
for Advent, Christmas, and Epiphany

COMPILED BY SARAH ARTHUR

PARACLETE PRESS
BREWSTER, MASSACHUSETTS

2014 First printing

Light Upon Light: A Literary Guide to Prayer for Advent, Christmas, and Epiphany

Copyright © 2014 by Sarah Arthur

ISBN 978-1-61261-419-9

Library of Congress Cataloging-in-Publication Data

Arthur, Sarah.
  Light upon light : a literary guide to prayer for Advent, Christmas, and Epiphany / compiled by Sarah Arthur.
      pages cm
  Includes index.
  ISBN 978-1-61261-419-9 (pb with french flaps)
  1. Epiphany season—Prayers and devotions. 2. Advent—Prayers and devotions. 3. Christmas—Prayers and devotions. I. Title.
  BV50.E7A78 2014
  242'.33—dc23   2014018529

10 9 8 7 6 5 4 3 2 1

Published by Paraclete Press
Brewster, Massachusetts
www.paracletepress.com
Printed in the United States of America

For Sam, whose early birth
put this project on precarious hold
—but whose advent brought joy nonetheless.
May you be a light-bearer, always.

They shall praise Thee and suffer in every generation
With glory and derision,
Light upon light, mounting the saints' stair.

—T. S. Eliot, from "A Song for Simeon"

CONTENTS

INTRODUCTION

WELCOME TO THIS LITERARY GUIDE TO PRAYER FOR THE SEASONS OF ADVENT, CHRISTMAS, AND EPIPHANY. For those familiar with the first collection, *At the Still Point: A Literary Guide to Prayer in Ordinary Time*, this book may feel like an old friend—not only its format but its aesthetic, the overall invitation to a companionship that delights. For those for whom such a prayer guide is new, come on in. Pull up a chair. You're in good company.

Many of us, when charting the timeline of our lives, can point to a moment when a story or poem *happened*. It happened the way an accident or a record-breaking snowfall happened: it was perhaps expected, perhaps not. One moment we were performing the usual routine—pouring cereal, say, or opening the mail—and the next moment we sat motionless with a book in our hands, eyes unfocused, a wave of words washing over us as relentlessly as a newsreel. When we look back and narrate our life, we will remember precisely where we were sitting, what we were wearing, the way the eaves dripped in the fog. Ever after, when we hear dripping eaves, we will remember. The story, the poem, will come back to us like the voice of long-dead grandfather, sharply, as if there has been no time or distance in between. It doesn't matter who wrote it, or why. What matters is that it changed us.

That is the gift of great literature, a gift that comes to us even at Christmas—when so much good art is effortlessly shoved aside in favor of the flashy, the cheap, the temporal. Finding the works for this collection, discovering some of these authors and poets, has been like lighting one candle after another. Flame upon flame, light upon light, until the hallowed sanctuary of our quiet devotion becomes something of a shrine.

Winter in the Northern Hemisphere is particularly suited for such encounters, and likewise suited to prayer and reflection. We find ourselves more and more indoors, ever in shadow, our bodies slowing to the rhythm of the sleeping woodlands. Silence is not hard to find. And yet crashing into the midwinter quiet comes the most frantic event of the cultural year. Perhaps it is our fear of stillness, of quiet, that drives us to anything but the "silent night" of Christmas: we do not want to know what we might discover in reflection. More likely it is a consumer economy that thrives on a relentless pace: slow and contemplative people are not shopping people; silence does not sell.

So the one time of year that we are given to pause and seek the One who seeks us becomes the one time of year that drives us nearly to self-extinction. And it is this season, of any, when we are least likely to pick up a book and read. Who has time for that? But it is a Word that has come to us, and words that tell the story of that Word from generation to generation. We risk, in our time, losing the words that truly have meaning, the stories and works of substance. What has been said before is said again, in ever more sentimental or sensational fashion—and set to pop music besides, which over time makes us immune.

Hence you hold, not just a guide to prayer, but a *literary* guide to prayer. Words of meaning, crafted to evoke a vision, or a truth, or both. Here you will find poetry, some of it familiar, much of it new, some of it in danger of being forgotten. Here are excerpts from classic and contemporary fiction, everything from fairytale to literary novella, discovered after many long months of hunting for something other than "'Twas the Night Before Christmas." New voices—old and young, female and male, multiethnic—invite you to experience Christmas in all its raw strangeness, stripped (when possible) of sentiment, tuned to a different pitch.

Some of the works in this collection are obviously seasonal, some obviously Christian. Others are neither. Still others face the darkness, dealing with the realities of a broken world. Take for instance, the Victorian obsession with death, particularly the death and suffering of small children. It is a theme we'd rather not think about at Christmas, when children—the hale and hearty—are lifted up, lavished like kings. And yet, written into the biblical birth narrative, into the celebration of a child born and flourishing and growing to manhood, is the story of the Holy Innocents, the infants and toddlers slaughtered in and around Bethlehem during Herod's quest to eliminate a threat. Art and culture that ignores this, particularly at Christmastime, is not honest.

Then there's the theme of the sojourner: the foreigner, the homeless, the outcast who seeks a place to rest in an often-hostile land. True: for a cultural minority there is no place like home for the holidays. But for many, many others—like the Holy Family itself—home is an elusive vision, complexified by relocation, or political asylum, or immigration, or domestic strife, or any number of social systems that bind and oppress. Travelers come following a Star but must leave for home by another road; some may never settle anywhere at all. These wandering voices, too, are part of the Christmas story and should not be neglected.

Other themes emerge, there to be discovered. They may touch you on this reading; they may not. And not every individual poem or story will suit your spiritual temperament. That is perfectly fine. Christmas will come again each year, and with it the opportunity to meet these writings with new vision, fresh insight, a year's worth of growing behind you. Allow them, if you will, to give the gift of themselves.

As I write early on this December morning, snow lies deep in my garden. Night retreats westward; stars slowly start to fade. Two small boys sleep across the hall, resting in the grace-filled inertia of the very young. Many, many things must be done today, not only to sustain a household but also to navigate the cultural expectations surrounding the coming holidays. But I will choose—if you do—to sit. I will choose to breathe in the words of others. Here in the dark I will seek points of light that cannot be extinguished, no matter how frenetic the world.

Our readings begin with the first Sunday of Advent, the start of the Christian New Year. On any other calendar there's nothing particularly notable about this day. It doesn't mark the solstice or some special phase of the moon. Rather, the Christian New Year begins on an obscure Sunday in early winter when we rise in the dark, bathe in the dark, dress and eat in the gloom of a gray dawn. It comes at a time when the Northern Hemisphere braces itself for a descent into the unlit, low-ceilinged root cellar of the year. We light a candle, peer into the hushed and cobwebbed darkness, step over the dusty detritus of old harvests. It will only get darker from here.

Perhaps that's why, of all the liturgical seasons, Advent was one of the last to be developed. Before Advent, before even Christmas, Christians were celebrating Epiphany—or the "day of manifestations"—on or around January 6 as early as the third century.[1] In secular contexts, an epiphany heralded the birth or visit of a king; in religious contexts, the appearance of the gods. For Christians, it spoke not only of the coming of foreign dignitaries who followed the light of an unusual star to the birthplace of an unusual king, but also of the revealing of Jesus at his nativity, his baptism, and his first miracle in the wedding at Cana. Light upon light, story upon story, manifesting the true nature of this God-man to the world. Liturgical stair-steps up and out of the cellar as the days already began to lengthen.

By the fourth century, the celebration of Christ's *mass*, the birth of Christ, had taken hold as a separate festival on or around December 25. Scholars are unclear as to why this date: it could very well have been a reaction to, or an appropriation of, the pagan solstice festivals taking place at that time. As the non-Christian world heralded "the birth of the invincible sun," the Christian community claimed the verse from Malachi 4:2, which promised that "the sun of righteousness shall rise, with healing in its wings."[2] More light, pouring forth into the gloom of the year.

As Christian theology developed, the larger mystery of the Incarnation—of God taking on human flesh—eventually became a touchstone for Christmas celebrations. Not only has God's chosen One appeared among us, blazing like the sun, but this One is God himself, bound up in our human mess, taking on our human suffering, living and dying as one of us. For Eastern churches, the Incarnation itself is what saves us: the Cross and Resurrection are merely part of a larger whole. When a holy God touched a corrupt humanity, God's goodness reversed our corruption, restored us to holiness. We were like a basket of rotten apples coming in contact with one good apple: not only did the good apple retain its essential goodness, but also it reversed the decay of all the rest. In the words of Saint John the Apostle, "The light shines in the darkness, and the darkness did not overcome it" (John 1:5).

So the light illumines the dank cellar of our human condition, and not surprisingly we find ourselves shrinking back, pulling into the shadows, suddenly aware of the dirt, the smudges, the overall ugliness of our own sinful selves. Thus comes Advent, the last of the three winter seasons to develop in the Christian calendar. It is a time of preparation leading to the appearance of the light. Indeed, for the early Christians it was a penitential season like Lent. You dared not approach the light without first searching your soul, cleaning up the mess, preparing yourself for its sanctifying presence.

During Advent we make way for the coming of a Savior for whom the world is not worthy. And not only that, but also we brace ourselves for his coming again in judgment one day. We rehearse both the first and second coming, juxtaposed against a backdrop of the world's longest night, all creation holding its breath for the final turn, the last and best sunrise.

So let it begin.

HOW TO USE THIS BOOK

This guide to prayer is divided into eighteen sections: four for the weeks of Advent, four for Christmastide (Christmas Eve, Christmas Day, and the two Sundays following, if applicable), and nine for the weeks of Epiphany, also known as the first and shortest season of Ordinary Time.[3] Each section begins with a suggested outline for daily prayer, including an opening prayer (generally taken from classic poetry), a psalm for the day or week, suggested Scriptures, five to seven literary readings, an opportunity for personal prayer and reflection, and a closing prayer (again, taken from classic poetry). As with *At the Still Point*, a theme for each section provides an organizing thought that holds it all together.

Begin your time of devotion each day or week with the opening prayer; then move on to the suggested psalm. It can be meditated upon daily, or you may wish to read only a portion of the psalm each day. Or find a particular section of the psalm with which you especially resonate and dwell there awhile, meditating on the words as a kind of personal prayer. The psalms as Hebrew poetry are some of the greatest literature you will encounter, providing echoes and resonances that a mere cursory skim will miss.

After the psalm, both the rest of the Scriptures and the readings can be read daily or spread throughout the week as a guide for prayerful reflection. As you may already have discovered, the medium of poetry lends itself rather well to this kind of meditation. It is nearly impossible to read a poem both quickly and well. Often we find ourselves reading it a second or even a third time, savoring its images, marveling at the crafted word patterns. It may not be all that difficult to imagine how to turn your poetic meditation into prayerful reflection, inviting God into your wonderings and insights. With the fiction excerpts, however, in many cases you will be jumping in midstory, with only a brief editor's note to orient you to people, places, and plot. It may take you a moment to settle in to the author's voice, to let the story weave its spell on your imagination.

That's why some of the excerpts are rather long, because fiction doesn't work its magic right away. You might consider picking a day in the week in which you will focus only on the story rather than trying to cram the other readings in as well. Meanwhile, you are absolved from trying to hunt for the story's "point." Some of the fiction may have obvious connections to the section's theme; others may not. Rather than agonize over an excerpt, it is perfectly okay to move on, trusting that if the Spirit has something to say to you (whether it has to do with the theme or not), the insight will come in time.

Once you have done the readings, there is an opportunity for personal prayer and reflection, whether through silence or journaling or whatever mode works for you (see the discussion of *lectio divina*, below, for more ideas). What jumped out at you from the readings? When did you sense God's presence? What might God be saying to you?

Finally, wrap up your time with the closing prayer.

Still unsure of how to engage fiction or poetry prayerfully? Consider applying aspects of the practice of *lectio divina* (divine reading) to this process. It is an ancient method for prayerful meditation on the Scriptures, involving four steps: *lectio* (reading the passage), *meditatio* (meditating; reading it over several more times slowly), *oratio* (letting the text speak to you by paying attention to words, phrases, images, or ideas), and *contemplatio* (shifting one's focus to God; resting in God's presence). To be clear, I recognize that these literary readings are not the words of Scripture. But the basic principles of *lectio* that one might apply to Scripture can be applied to novels and poetry—since Scripture is, among other things, great literature.

We have already mentioned the opportunity for personal prayer and reflection that follows the readings. This is the *oratio* and *contemplatio* stage. You have read the passage (*lectio*)—perhaps several times, slowly (*meditatio*)—and now you go back through it, making note of the words, phrases, images, metaphors, or ideas that "shimmer." What jumps out at you? What speaks to you (*oratio*)? You may even want to write it down. Then invite God to show you why this word or phrase spoke so strongly. What is God up to? In what ways do you sense God's presence in the midst of this reading? Finally, pause and simply rest in that presence (*contemplatio*). There are no demands on you in this moment. You are simply resting in God.

Dwell in the light.

ADVENT WEEK 1

Begin with a Change

OPENING PRAYER

Of the Father's love begotten,
Ere the worlds began to be,
He is Alpha and Omega,
He the source, the ending He,
Of the things that are,
That have been,
And that future years shall see,
Evermore and evermore!
—Translated from a poem by AURELIUS PRUDENTIUS
(Roman, ca. AD 348–415)[4]

SCRIPTURES

PSALM 24 | ISAIAH 43:15–21 | ROMANS 8:18–25 | JOHN 1:1–9

READINGS

"Conversion" by MARCI JOHNSON
"The Beginning of the World" by SCOTT CAIRNS
"Incarnation" by AMIT MAJMUDAR
"Freeman Creek Grove" by PAUL WILLIS
"Later Life: A Double Sonnet of Sonnets (XIX)" by CHRISTINA ROSSETTI
"Advent in Michigan" by SARAH ARTHUR
From *Godric* by FREDERICK BUECHNER

PERSONAL PRAYER AND REFLECTION

CLOSING PRAYER

Christ, to Thee with God the Father,
And, O Holy Ghost, to Thee,
Hymn and chant with high thanksgiving,
And unwearied praises be:
> Honor, glory, and dominion,
> And eternal victory,

> > Evermore and evermore!

—Translated from a poem by AURELIUS PRUDENTIUS
(Roman, ca. AD 348–415)

READINGS

Conversion
MARCI JOHNSON (American, contemporary)

John 1:14

How can word
become flesh?
Belly. Bone.

Tongue—the feel
in the mouth a word
rolling around. Word,

not a kiss not the thing
itself—a name. The arch
of a foot. Your face

in my hands, just
a name. Blue sky lolling
beyond the window

frame—eyes open.
Just a way of looking.
Begin with a change.

————

The Beginning of the World

SCOTT CAIRNS (American, contemporary)

In the midst of His long and silent observation of eternal presence, during which He, now and again, would find His own attention spiraling in that abysmal soup, God draws up what He will call His voice from unfathomable slumber where it lay in that great, sepulchral Throat and out from Him, in what would thereafter be witnessed as a gesture of pouring, falls the Word, as a bright, translucent gem among primal turbulence, still spinning. Think this is the evening? Well, that was night. And born into that turmoil so bright or so dark as to render all points moot, God's pronouncement and first measure.

But before even that original issue, first utterance of our Great Solitary, His self-demarcation of Himself, before even that first birth I suspect an inclination. In God's center, something of a murmur, pre-verbal, pre-phenomenal, perhaps nothing more disturbing to the moment than a silent clearing of the hollowed throat, an approach merely, but it was a beginning earlier than the one we had supposed, and a willingness for something standing out apart from Him, if nonetheless His own.

Still, by the time anything so weakly theatrical as that has occurred, already so many invisible preparations: God's general availability, His brooding peckishness, an appetite and predilection—even before invention—to invent, to give vent, an all but unsuspected longing for desire followed by the eventual arrival of desire's deep hum, its thrumming escalation and upward flight into the dome's aperture, already open and voluble and without warning given voice.

But how long, and without benefit of Time's secretarial skills, had that Visage lain facing our direction? What hunger must have built before the first repast? And, we might well ask, to what end, if any? And if any end, why begin? (The imagination's tedious mimesis of the sea.) In the incommensurate cathedral of Himself, what stillness?

What extreme expression could prevail against that self-same weight? And would such, then, be approximate to trinity? An organization, say, like this: The Enormity, Its Aspirations, Its Voice. Forever God and the mind of God in wordless discourse until that first polarity divests a shout against the void. Perhaps it is that first resounding measure which lays foundation for every flowing utterance to come. It would appear to us, I suppose, as a chaos of waters—and everything since proceeding from the merest drop of it.

So long as we have come this far, we may as well continue onto God's initial venture, His first concession at that locus out of time when He invented the absence of Himself, which first retraction avails for all the cosmos and for us. In the very midst of His unending wholeness He withdraws, and a portion of what He was He abdicates. We may suppose our entire aberration to proceed from that dislocated Hand, and may suppose the terror we suspect— which lingers if only to discourage too long an entertainment—to be trace and resonance of that self-inflicted wound.

So why the vertiginous kiss of waters? Why the pouring chaos at our beginning, which charges all that scene with . . . would you call it *rapture*? Perhaps the dawning impulse of our creation, meager as it may have been, pronounced—in terms we never heard—God's return.

———

"Incarnation" FROM the poem cycle *Seventeens*
AMIT MAJMUDAR (Indian-American, contemporary)

Inheart yourself, immensity. Immarrow,
Embone, enrib yourself. The wind won't borrow
A plane, nor water climb aboard a current,
But you be all we are, and all we aren't.
You rigged this whirligig, you make it run:
Stop juggling atoms and oppose your thumbs.
That's what we like, we like our rich to slum.
The rich, it may be, like it too. Enmeat
Yourself so we can rise onto our feet
And meet. For eyes, just take two suns and shrink them.
Make all your thoughts as small as you can think them.
Encrypt in flesh, enigma, what we can't
Quite English. We will almost understand.
If there are things for which we don't have clearance,
There's secrecy aplenty in appearance.
Face it, another word for skin is hide.
Show me the face that never lied.

———

Freeman Creek Grove
PAUL WILLIS (American, contemporary)

(*Sequoia gigantea*)

Hiking down November snow,
we saw the first one still below us,
mounding up like a juniper
in the Shasta fir and the sugar pine.

Soon the trail entered its presence
(with Thanksgiving a day behind),

the trunk rising in dusky red, in fluted columns
strangely soft to our curious touch.

The first branches began at the tops
of other trees and continued into familiar wonder,
older perhaps than the Incarnation,
and longer rooted, and while they are here,
shedding for us new mercy of cones
flung green and small on the white of our steps.

We girdled the trunk with open arms,
unable to circumference it, much less
to find its center. In our random cries,
in the things we said to our wandering children,
I heard proclamation of peace on earth,
a wooden promise kept fresh for millennia,
the inaudible sound of a secret
seed in the South Sierra where eagles
nest in the falling snow.

———

Later Life: A Double Sonnet of Sonnets (XIX)
CHRISTINA ROSSETTI (English, 1830–1894)

Here now is Winter. Winter, after all,
   Is not so drear as was my boding dream
   While Autumn gleamed its last watery gleam
On sapless leafage too inert to fall.
Still leaves and berries clothe my garden wall
   Where ivy thrives on scantiest sunny beam;
   Still here a bud and there a blossom seem
Hopeful, and robin still is musical.
Leaves, flowers and fruit and one delightful song

Remain; these days are short, but now the nights
Intense and long, hang out their utmost lights;
Such starry nights are long, yet not too long;
Frost nips the weak, while strengthening still the strong
Against that day when Spring sets all to rights.

———

Advent in Michigan
SARAH ARTHUR (American, contemporary)

In time
the sons of men filled the earth
with their evil deeds.
And God beheld the desolate wastes
the soiled streets
the bitter brown of barren fields
and the sin of the world
cut him to the heart.

"I will blot from the earth
the memory of these things.
Behold, I will make all things new!"
So he gathered up clouds
from the four corners of the sky,
billows pregnant with promise.
He gathered them in great, dark piles
on the horizon of hills
while the weathermen watched
grandmothers gazed
schoolchildren pressed their noses against the glass.

And God said,
"Let there be snow."

First, small white flakes
like lace, drifting.

Then—wind
driving snow before it, a blizzard
hiding hills from view
(and the tops of church steeples
and street lights, too).

For forty days
the land was covered in white,
the wretched lines of a wretched world
blurred soft overnight—

buried, forgotten

        as God birthed grace upon the earth.

———

FROM *Godric*

FREDERICK BUECHNER (American, contemporary)

[Editor's note: As a foil to classic hagiography in which saints are practically faultless, Buechner gives twelfth-century Saint Godric his own rough, humorous, and thoroughly honest voice. In this excerpt Godric is now an elderly hermit living near the River Wear in medieval England, attended by the monks Perkin and Reginald.]

Bishop Pudsey summons me to Christmas mass at Durham. I think he means in part to honor me, in part to bring some kind of honor on himself by fishing up old Godric none have seen away from Wear for twenty years and more. I can scarcely hobble with a stick. The weather's foul. I'd sooner have a barber draw my three or four last teeth than go. But Reginald says I must for Jesu's sake. Even Perkin chides. He says, "What good is it to live a hundred years, old man, if no one gets a chance to gawk at you but rats and owls?" So in the end I go. My peace goes too.

"First we'll have to swab you down," says Perkin. "Else they'll think it's not a man we've brought to mass but the ancient, mildewed carcass of a bear."

Then he and Reginald fetch a pail or two of Wear and warm them by the fire. I've worn my clothes so long they cleave to me and fall apart as I am stripped. They scrub me clean as if to lay me in my tomb. They free my hair of knots and comb the cobwebs out. Perkin says they find mouse droppings in it and a spider's nest. They trim my beard. They pare my nails. They sprinkle me with rosewater like a bride and deck me out in garments fresh. I let them set aside my iron vest so I can move more easily, but when they try to place a pair of sandals on my feet, I balk. For fifty years or more I've gone unshod. I won't change now.

They load me on a cart made soft with straw, and Perkin sits astride the mule. Reginald tramps along beside to catch me should the jouncing jounce me off. Snow falls. The sky is grey. The air is damp and chill. On such a day as this, I think, our Savior first saw light while, all about the manger, beasts knelt down to worship him.

When we enter Durham's gate, folk gather in the streets to see me pass. Some ask my blessing, and I raise a hand so milky clean I hardly know it's mine to sign them with the cross. Some snatch at bits of straw as charms against the evil eye. A fat man tries to cut a snippet from my cloak. I catch him in the belly with my heel. Bells ring. Dogs bark. A child makes water in the street. Women lean from windows, waving flags.

A blind man in a bonnet, led by friends, begs me to touch his eyes that he may see. I place my thumbs on them. His lids go flitter-flutter, but I mark no greater change in him. He gropes to find his friends again. They catch him when he stumbles on a stone. Some bring me gifts. A pot of honey. A kerchief worked in silk. A basket with a guinea-fowl that struggles free and flaps off cackling through the air. They shove and stomp to touch my clothes. I close my eyes and pray.

Dear Father, see how these thy children hunger here. They starve for want of what they cannot name. Their poor souls are famished. Their foolish hands reach out. Oh grant them richer fare than one old sack of bones whose wits begin to turn. Feed them with something more than Godric here, for Godric's no less starved for thee than they. Have mercy, Lord. Amen.

ADVENT WEEK 2

Annunciations

OPENING PRAYER

Deliver us for Thy descent
Into the Virgin, whose womb was a place
  Of middle kind; and Thou being sent
To ungracious us, stayed'st at her full of grace. . . .
—JOHN DONNE (English, 1572–1631)

SCRIPTURES

PSALM 111 | 1 SAMUEL 2:1–10 | 1 JOHN 1:1–4 | LUKE 1:26–38

READINGS

"Flight" by JEANNE MURRAY WALKER
"Mary and Gabriel" by RUPERT BROOKE
"Annunciation" by ELIZABETH B. ROONEY
"Annunciation" by JOHN DONNE
"Magnificat" by MARY F. C. PRATT
From *Silas Marner* by GEORGE ELIOT

PERSONAL PRAYER AND REFLECTION

CLOSING PRAYER

. . . And through Thy poor birth, where first Thou
    Glorified'st poverty,
And yet soon after riches didst allow,
By accepting King's gifts in the Epiphany,
Deliver, and make us, to both ways free.
—JOHN DONNE (English, 1572–1631)

❦

READINGS

Flight

JEANNE MURRAY WALKER (American, contemporary)

The angel speeding down the runway pulls up
her wing flaps, and, wouldn't you know it, wobbles,
then dribbles to a stop. She stands on the windy
tarmac, embarrassed, brushing her blond hair
from her eyes, trying to remember how to elevate
herself, wishing she'd worn jeans instead of
the girly skirt that works for flying. It's gravity's old
malice, showing up in the strangest places,
for instance at the corner where the fortune cookie truck
forgets how to turn, tipping gracefully, sliding on
its side as cookies spill into the summer night.
Around the city good luck stalls, turning us into

bodies, just protoplasm for a wasp to sing.
Even love is a sad mechanical business then,
and prayer an accumulation of words I would kill
to believe in. There's no happy end to a poem
that lacks faith, no way to get out. I could
mention that doubt—no doubt—is a testing. Meanwhile
our angel glances toward the higher power,
wondering how much help she'll get, not a manual,
for sure, but a pause in entropy perhaps, until she
can get her wings scissoring. Call it cooperation,
how a rise can build, sustain itself, and lift her
past the tree line. Then she knows she won't
fall, oh holy night, *can't* fall. Anything but.

Mary and Gabriel
RUPERT BROOKE (English, 1887–1915)

Young Mary, loitering once her garden way,
Felt a warm splendor grow in the April day,
As wine that blushes water through. And soon,
Out of the gold air of the afternoon,
One knelt before her: hair he had, or fire,
Bound back above his ears with golden wire,
Baring the eager marble of his face.
Not man's nor woman's was the immortal grace
Rounding the limbs beneath that robe of white,
And lighting the proud eyes with changeless light,
Incurious. Calm as his wings, and fair,
That presence filled the garden.
                              She stood there,
Saying, "What would you, Sir?"
                              He told his word,
"Blessed art thou of women!" Half she heard,
Hands folded and face bowed, half long had known,
The message of that clear and holy tone,
That fluttered hot sweet sobs about her heart;
Such serene tidings moved such human smart.
Her breath came quick as little flakes of snow.
Her hands crept up her breast. She did but know
It was not hers. She felt a trembling stir
Within her body, a will too strong for her
That held and filled and mastered all. With eyes
Closed, and a thousand soft short broken sighs,
She gave submission; fearful, meek, and glad.

She wished to speak. Under her breasts she had
Such multitudinous burnings, to and fro,
And throbs not understood; she did not know

If they were hurt or joy for her; but only
That she was grown strange to herself, half lonely,
All wonderful, filled full of pains to come
And thoughts she dare not think, swift thoughts and dumb,
Human, and quaint, her own, yet very far,
Divine, dear, terrible, familiar . . .
Her heart was faint for telling; to relate
Her limbs' sweet treachery, her strange high estate,
Over and over, whispering, half revealing,
Weeping; and so find kindness to her healing.
'Twixt tears and laughter, panic hurrying her,
She raised her eyes to that fair messenger.
He knelt unmoved, immortal; with his eyes
Gazing beyond her, calm to the calm skies;
Radiant, untroubled in his wisdom, kind.
His sheaf of lilies stirred not in the wind.
How should she, pitiful with mortality,
Try the wide peace of that felicity
With ripples of her perplexed shaken heart,
And hints of human ecstasy, human smart,
And whispers of the lonely weight she bore,
And how her womb within was hers no more
And at length hers?
                    Being tired, she bowed her head;
And said, "So be it!"
                    The great wings were spread
Showering glory on the fields, and fire.
The whole air, singing, bore him up, and higher,
Unswerving, unreluctant. Soon he shone
A gold speck in the gold skies; then was gone.

The air was colder, and grey. She stood alone.

Annunciation

ELIZABETH B. ROONEY (American, 1924–1999)

There was
Is
Has been
And will be
An everywhere
Fixed
And transfixed
Within
That point in time
Wherein
One single
Simple
Open soul
Received
The potency
Of the creative whole.

————

Annunciation

JOHN DONNE (English, 1572–1631)

Salvation to all that will is nigh;
That All, which always is all everywhere,
Which cannot sin, and yet all sins must bear,
Which cannot die, yet cannot choose but die,
Lo! faithful Virgin, yields Himself to lie
In prison, in thy womb; and though He there
Can take no sin, nor thou give, yet He'll wear,
Taken from thence, flesh, which death's force may try.
Ere by the spheres time was created, thou

Wast in His mind, who is thy Son, and Brother;
Whom thou conceiv'st, conceived; yea, thou art now
Thy Maker's maker, and thy Father's mother,
Thou hast light in dark, and shutt'st in little room
Immensity cloister'd in thy dear womb.

———

Magnificat
MARY F. C. PRATT (American, contemporary)

Under pine trees in the snow,
the chickadees around my head,
I wept for the will of God,
this hungry woman fed.
All the shadows shifted
while my back was turned.
Once and always on my finger
one soft and small gray bird.
Not a twisting
due to prayer,
but all its own,
and mine together.
And so I bear the gift,
carry it through time—
this deepest darkness,
astonishing grace.

———

FROM *Silas Marner*

GEORGE ELIOT (a.k.a. Mary Ann Evans; English, 1819–1880)

[Editor's note: Near the provincial village of Raveloe lives a mysterious outsider, Silas Marner the weaver, who arrived from parts unknown many years ago and has lived a hermit's life ever since. But recently his treasure of earnings was stolen, throwing him into the company of his fellow humans, one of whom—the kindly Dolly Winthrop—pays him a visit with her small son, Aaron. Her gentle but direct encouragement speaks to the change that is coming, that has already begun, in his lonely life.]

They had to knock loudly before Silas heard them; but when he did come to the door he showed no impatience, as he would once have done, at a visit that had been unasked for and unexpected. Formerly, his heart had been as a locked casket with its treasure inside; but now the casket was empty, and the lock was broken. Left groping in darkness, with his prop utterly gone, Silas had inevitably a sense, though a dull and half-despairing one, that if any help came to him it must come from without; and there was a slight stirring of expectation at the sight of his fellow-men, a faint consciousness of dependence on their goodwill. He opened the door wide to admit Dolly, but without otherwise returning her greeting than by moving the armchair a few inches as a sign that she was to sit down in it. Dolly, as soon as she was seated, removed the white cloth that covered her lard-cakes, and said in her gravest way—

"I'd a baking yisterday, Master Marner, and the lard-cakes turned out better nor common, and I'd ha' asked you to accept some, if you'd thought well. I don't eat such things myself, for a bit o' bread's what I like from one year's end to the other; but men's stomichs are made so comical, they want a change—they do, I know, God help 'em."

Dolly sighed gently as she held out the cakes to Silas, who thanked her kindly and looked very close at them, absently, being accustomed to look so at everything he took into his hand—eyed all the while by the wondering bright orbs of the small Aaron, who had made an outwork of his mother's chair, and was peeping round from behind it.

"There's letters pricked on 'em," said Dolly. "I can't read 'em myself, and there's nobody, not Mr. Macey himself, rightly knows what they mean; but they've a good meaning, for they're the same as is on the pulpit-cloth at church. What are they, Aaron, my dear?"

Aaron retreated completely behind his outwork.

"Oh, go, that's naughty," said his mother, mildly. "Well, whativer the letters are, they've a good meaning; and it's a stamp as has been in our house, Ben says, ever since he was a little un, and his mother used to put it on the cakes, and I've allays put it on too; for if there's any good, we've need of it i' this world."

"It's I. H. S.,"[5] said Silas, at which proof of learning Aaron peeped round the chair again.

"Well, to be sure, you can read 'em off," said Dolly. "Ben's read 'em to me many and many a time, but they slip out o' my mind again; the more's the pity, for they're good letters, else they wouldn't be in the church; and so I prick 'em on all the loaves and all the cakes, though sometimes they won't hold, because o' the rising—for, as I said, if there's any good to be got we've need of it i' this world—that we have; and I hope they'll bring good to you, Master Marner, for it's wi' that will I brought you the cakes; and you see the letters have held better nor common."

Silas was as unable to interpret the letters as Dolly, but there was no possibility of misunderstanding the desire to give comfort that made itself heard in her quiet tones. He said, with more feeling than before—"Thank you—thank you kindly." But he laid down the cakes and seated himself absently—drearily unconscious of any distinct benefit towards which the cakes and the letters, or even Dolly's kindness, could tend for him.

"Ah, if there's good anywhere, we've need of it," repeated Dolly, who did not lightly forsake a serviceable phrase. She looked at Silas pityingly as she went on. "But you didn't hear the church-bells this morning, Master Marner? I doubt you didn't know it was Sunday. Living so lone here, you lose your count, I daresay; and then, when your loom makes a noise, you can't hear the bells, more partic'lar now the frost kills the sound."

"Yes, I did; I heard 'em," said Silas, to whom Sunday bells were a mere accident of the day, and not part of its sacredness. There had been no bells in Lantern Yard.

"Dear heart!" said Dolly, pausing before she spoke again. "But what a pity it is you should work of a Sunday, and not clean yourself—if you *didn't* go to church; for if you'd a roasting bit, it might be as you couldn't leave it, being a lone man. But there's the bakehus, if you could make up your mind to spend a twopence on the oven now and then,—not every week, in course—I shouldn't like to do that myself,—you might carry your bit o' dinner there, for it's nothing but right to have a bit o' summat hot of a Sunday, and not to make it as you can't know your dinner from Saturday. But now, upo' Christmas-day, this blessed Christmas as is ever coming, if you was to take your dinner to the bakehus, and go to church, and see the holly and the yew, and hear the anthim, and then take the sacramen', you'd be a deal the better, and you'd know which end you stood on, and you could put your trust i' Them as knows better nor we do, seein' you'd ha' done what it lies on us all to do."

Dolly's exhortation, which was an unusually long effort of speech for her, was uttered in the soothing persuasive tone with which she would have tried to prevail on a sick man to take his medicine, or a basin of gruel for which he had no appetite. Silas had never before been closely urged on the point of his absence from church, which had only been thought of as a part of his general queerness; and he was too direct and simple to evade Dolly's appeal.

"Nay, nay," he said, "I know nothing o' church. I've never been to church."

"No!" said Dolly, in a low tone of wonderment. Then bethinking herself of Silas's advent from an unknown country, she said, "Could it ha' been as they'd no church where you was born?"

"Oh, yes," said Silas, meditatively, sitting in his usual posture of leaning on his knees, and supporting his head. "There was churches—a many—it was a big town. But I knew nothing of 'em—I went to chapel."

Dolly was much puzzled at this new word, but she was rather afraid of inquiring further, lest "chapel" might mean some haunt of wickedness. After a little thought, she said—

"Well, Master Marner, it's niver too late to turn over a new leaf, and if you've niver had no church, there's no telling the good it'll do you. For I feel so set up and comfortable as niver was, when I've been and heard the prayers, and the singing to the praise and glory o' God, as Mr. Macey gives out—and Mr. Crackenthorp saying good words, and more partic'lar on Sacramen' Day; and if a bit o' trouble comes, I feel as I can put up wi' it, for I've looked for help i' the right quarter, and gev myself up to Them as we must all give ourselves up to at the last; and if we'n done our part, it isn't to be believed as Them as are above us 'ull be worse nor we are, and come short o' Their'n."

ADVENT WEEK 3

Sojourners in the Land

OPENING PRAYER

Lead, Kindly Light, amid the circling gloom,
  Lead Thou me on!
The night is dark, and I am far from home—
  Lead Thou me on!
Keep Thou my feet; I do not ask to see
The distant scene,—one step enough for me.
—JOHN HENRY, CARDINAL NEWMAN (English, 1801–1890)

SCRIPTURES

PSALM 137 | JEREMIAH 31:7–14 | EPHESIANS 2:11–22 | LUKE 2:1–7

READINGS

"The House of Christmas" by G. K. CHESTERTON
"Bethlehem, Indiana" by SUSANNA CHILDRESS
"Upon Christ His Birth" by SIR JOHN SUCKLING
"The Eternal Son" by LI-YOUNG LEE
From *The Wednesday Wars* by GARY D. SCHMIDT

PERSONAL PRAYER AND REFLECTION

CLOSING PRAYER

So long Thy power hath blest me, sure it still
  Will lead me on,
O'er moor and fen, o'er crag and torrent, till
  The night is gone;

And with the morn those angel faces smile
Which I have loved long since, and lost awhile.
—JOHN HENRY, CARDINAL NEWMAN (English, 1801–1890)

READINGS

The House of Christmas
G. K. CHESTERTON (English, 1874–1936)

There fared a mother driven forth
Out of an inn to roam;
In the place where she was homeless
All men are at home.
The crazy stable close at hand,
With shaking timber and shifting sand,
Grew a stronger thing to abide and stand
Than the square stones of Rome.

For men are homesick in their homes,
And strangers under the sun,
And they lay their heads in a foreign land
Whenever the day is done.
Here we have battle and blazing eyes,
And chance and honor and high surprise,
But our homes are under miraculous skies
Where the Yule tale was begun.

A Child in a foul stable,
Where the beasts feed and foam;
Only where He was homeless
Are you and I at home;

We have hands that fashion and heads that know,
But our hearts we lost—how long ago!
In a place no chart nor ship can show
Under the sky's dome.

This world is wild as an old wives' tale,
And strange the plain things are,
The earth is enough and the air is enough
For our wonder and our war;
But our rest is as far as the fire-drake swings
And our peace is put in impossible things
Where clashed and thundered unthinkable wings
Round an incredible star.

To an open house in the evening
Home shall men come,
To an older place than Eden
And a taller town than Rome.
To the end of the way of the wandering star,
To the things that cannot be and that are,
To the place where God was homeless
And all men are at home.

———

Bethlehem, Indiana

SUSANNA CHILDRESS (American, contemporary)

Which glacier faltered in silencing your hills, Bethlehem?
Which Shawnee woman foraged your wild gooseberries? Where
but a knell of spruce and flowering dogwood, the smallest of starlings
crossing the Ohio River to a province once known as Ken-tah-ten,
could we find cascading-haired Mary, whose fingers hover

the unquestionable beauty of her new son's thighs, their tender fat
rolling, their slight spoonful of tendons kicking with the certainty
of impulse, unknown to him yet as the body's subtlest joy. No heifer
lows against her bale, for this is the Midwest, and our cows
are happy cows. But Mother & child are not in the barn, its rafters

housing a dozen fidgeting pigeons, nor are they in the east shed
where the combine neighbors the chicken coop. Say we were
to come upon these two as they share a moment while Joseph, who,
according to St. Brigit's account, cannot keep their only candle lit
and so has stepped away to shake his lighter, slap its plastic

shell against his jeans: you would realize, then, from the marquee
illuminating NO next to VACANCY, visible from the palm-sized
    window
eye-high in the custodian's closet, that you've found them in the Motel 6,
or perhaps its periphery, since there's no faded bedspread here, no bed,
no lamp, no faucet or sink, no folded white washcloth, the undulating

highway nearer to them than the front desk, whose single geranium
slouches toward discolor. Yes, it's Mary, and though her belly
no longer bulges with the full moon, she still shimmers, should you
look closely. Should you look closely you'd see the gray heads
of four mops gathered on the cement floor as bedding for this child,

whose mother has swabbed off most of the vernix caseosa covering
his body, whose firetruck-bespeckled swaddling has come undone,
and whose tiny fist knocks the mop handles set against the plastic
yellow placard that reads ¡CUIDADO! PISO MOJADO. Certainly,
    you think,
I'll be careful, but what you truly want is *answers*. Why the girl

so placid, soft strains of a Magnificat hushing her infant, why
her fiancée so stupefied by the brightest star he's ever seen
directly above them, and why O why the peacock farm

two miles south whose caretaker awakened with a sudden urge
for green bean casserole only to find a heavenly host inside

his refrigerator, which, incidentally, set off the fire alarm
and his wife in her cotton gown and rollers so that at this very minute
he's tying his boots, urging on her a robe for a trip up the road
to see what can be seen. Don't think the crickets for miles around
have shushed, or crawdads in their underground warren have ceased

to battle. The deer still turn their umber necks to listen before
disappearing into a thick of Beech trees and bubbles still rise
from the creek bed where podgy catfish switch their whiskers over
pebbles, a trellis of algae, a lost, sunken shoe. At this point, so few
know the unutterable brilliance of this night, that God would suffuse

the simple, the absolutely ordinary, indeed, the profane, with *the sacred*
that it's almost as if it hasn't happened. Only, it has, and the complex
   beauty
of all this might mean has found its shape, for a moment, in the sharp
cry let loose from a baby's mouth searching out the air around it
for his mother's breast. Perhaps the wind knows as it scoops through

the hollows of this place and more thinly matches the high, distant pitch
of human need and desire. For the wind has been across the river
into bluegrass country, 40 miles southeast of here to another
   Bethlehem,
and to the nineteen other states with at least one town called *Bet
   lechem*,
House of Bread—to Connecticut, Georgia, South Dakota, Texas,

New York, Louisiana, New Hampshire, Arizona, Iowa—where someone
not so long ago figured the final resting place of Rachel, the birthplace
of David, might make a nice name for their town. And when we,
who are not as deft or lissome as the wind, get turned around by a
   similar
copse of spruce wood, another field of harvested soybean, we'll

pull into the Quick-Mart for directions. The man at the counter whose young wife has just brought in her infant son for a visit won't look up when the bell over the door jangles our arrival, not at least, until he notices our faces, which are either somber or exultant as we say, *We're just passin' through* or *We've come to see—*

———

Upon Christ His Birth
SIR JOHN SUCKLING (English, 1609–1642)

Strange news! a city full? Will none give way
To lodge a guest that comes not every day?
No inn, nor tavern void? Yet I descry
One empty place alone, where we may lie:
In too much fullness is some want: but where?
Men's empty hearts: let's ask for lodging there.
But if they not admit us, then we'll say
Their hearts, as well as inns, are made of clay.

———

The Eternal Son
LI-YOUNG LEE (Asian-American, contemporary)

Someone's thinking about his mother tonight.

The wakeful son
of a parent who hardly sleeps,

the sleepless father of his own
restless child, God, is it you?
Is it me? Do you have a mother?

Who mixes flour and sugar
for your birthday cake?

Who stirs slumber and remembrance
in a song for your bedtime?

If you're the cry enjoining dawn,
who birthed you?

If you're the bell tolling night
without circumference, who rocked you?
Someone's separating
the white grains of his insomnia
from the black seeds
of his sleep.

If it isn't you, God, it must be me.

My mother's eternal son,
I can't hear the rain without thinking
it's her in the next room
folding our clothes to lay inside a suitcase.

And now she's counting her money
on the bed, the good paper
and the paper from the other country
in separate heaps.

If day comes soon, she could buy our passage.
But if our lot is the rest of the night,
we'll have to trust unseen hands
to hand us toward ever deeper sleep.

Then I'll be the crumb
at the bottom of her pocket,
and she can keep me
or sow me on the water,
as she pleases. Anyway,

she has too much to carry, she who knows
night must tell the rest of every story.

Now she's wondering about the sea.
She can't tell if the white foam laughs
I was born dark! while it spins
opposite the momentum of our dying,
or do the waves journey beyond
the name of every country
and the changing color of her hair.

And if she's weeping,
it's because she's misplaced
both our childhoods.

And if she's humming, it's because
she's heard the name of life:
A name, but no name, the dove

bereft of memory and finally singing
how the light happened
to one who gave up
ever looking back.

———

FROM *The Wednesday Wars*
GARY D. SCHMIDT (American, contemporary)

[Editor's note: In Schmidt's Newbery Honor Book, we experience
Christmas 1967 on Long Island through the eyes of seventh grader
Holling Hoodhood. Tensions are high in the ethnically diverse
community. For folks like Mrs. Bigio in the school cafeteria, whose
husband is killed in Vietnam, and Mai Thi, a Vietnamese refugee,
the holiday is less than happy. On the winter night Holling stars as
Ariel—complete with yellow tights and feathers—in a community

production of Shakespeare's *The Tempest*, he is snubbed by famous ballplayer Mickey Mantle, who refuses to sign Holling's baseball because of the tights. Even the kindness of his friends the Hupfers and of Mr. Goldman, the play's director, can't erase the pain.]

When gods die, they die hard. It's not like they fade away, or grow old, or fall asleep. They die in fire and pain, and when they come out of you, they leave your guts burned. It hurts more than anything you can talk about. And maybe worst of all is, you're not sure if there will ever be another god to fill their place. Or if you'd ever want another god to fill their place. You don't want fire to go out inside you twice.

The Hupfers drove me back to the Festival Theater. I went in to see if the men's dressing room was unlocked. It was, and Mr. Goldman was holding forth.

"My dainty Ariel!" he called, and threw his arms out wide, and the company—the men, that is, for the record—all clapped. "Where have you been? You, the star of the Extravaganza? Something should be wrong?"

I shook my head. How could you tell Mr. Goldman that the gods had died, when they lived so strongly in him? "Was 't well done?" I asked.

"Bravely, my diligence. Thou shalt be free."

And I was. I changed, and left the yellow tights with the feathers on the butt in a locker. Mr. Goldman told me I should stop by the bakery for some cream puffs "which will cost you not a thing," and I left. That was it. Outside, it was the first really cold night of winter, and the only fire in sight was the stars high above us and far away, glittering like ice.

The Hupfers were waiting, and drove me home.

We still didn't talk. Not the whole way.

When I got back, my parents were in the den watching television. It was so cold, the furnace was on high. The hot air tinkled the silver bells that decorated the white artificial Christmas tree that never dropped a single pine needle in the Perfect House.

"You're done earlier than I thought," my father said. "Bing Crosby is just about to start 'White Christmas,' as soon as this commercial is over."

"How did it go, Holling?" said my mother.

"Fine."

"I hope Mr. Goldman was happy with what you did," said my father.

"He said it was just swell."

"Good."

I went upstairs. The crooning notes of Bing Crosby's treetops glistening and children listening and sleigh bells in the snow followed me.

Just swell.

Happy holidays.

When we got back to school on Monday, there were only three more days before the holiday break. They were supposed to be a relaxed three days. Most teachers coasted through them, figuring that no one was going to learn all that much just before vacation. And they had to leave time for holiday parties on the last day, and making presents for each other, and for looking out the window, hoping for the miracle of snow on Long Island.

Even the lunches were supposed to have something special to them, like some kind of cake with thick white frosting, or pizza that actually had some cheese on it, or hamburgers that hadn't been cooked as thin as a record. Maybe something chocolate on the side.

But Mrs. Bigio wasn't interested in chocolate these days. It could have been the last holidays the planet was ever going to celebrate, and you wouldn't have known it from what Mrs. Bigio cooked for Camillo Junior High's lunch. It was Something Surprise every day, except that after the first day it wasn't Something Surprise anymore, because we knew what was coming. It was just Something.

But I didn't complain. I remembered the Wednesday afternoon Mrs. Bigio had come into Mrs. Baker's classroom and the sound of her sadness, and I knew what burned guts felt like.

Everyone else didn't complain because they were afraid to. You don't complain when Mrs. Bigio stares at you as you're going through the lunch line, with her hands on her hips and her hairnet pulled tight. You don't complain.

Not even when she spreads around her own happy holiday greetings.

"Take it and eat it," she said to Danny Hupfer when his hand hesitated over the Something.

"You're not supposed to examine it," she said to Meryl Lee, who was trying to figure out the Surprise part.

"You waiting for another cream puff?" she said to me. "Don't count on it this millennium."

And, on the last day before the holiday break, to Mai Thi: "Pick it up and be glad you're getting it. You shouldn't even be here, sitting like a queen in a refugee home while American boys are sitting in swamps on Christmas Day. They're the ones who should be here. Not you."

Mai Thi took her Something. She looked down, and kept going.

She probably didn't see that Mrs. Bigio was pulling her hairnet down lower over her face, because she was almost crying.

And probably Mrs. Bigio didn't see that Mai Thi was almost crying, too.

But I did. I saw them. And I wondered how many gods were dying in both of them right then, and whether any of them could be saved.

ADVENT WEEK 4

The Strange Guest

SCRIPTURES
PSALM 99 | ISAIAH 40:1–11 | HEBREWS 12:18–29 | JOHN 1:10–18

READINGS
"Writing a Sermon, December 23" by MARY F. C. PRATT
"Advent" by SUZANNE UNDERWOOD RHODES
"Mañana (Tomorrow)" by LOPE DE VEGA
"Nativity of Our Lord and Savior Jesus Christ" by CHRISTOPHER SMART
"Nativity" by LI-YOUNG LEE
From *A Christmas Carol* by CHARLES DICKENS

PERSONAL PRAYER AND REFLECTION

⁘

READINGS

Writing a Sermon, December 23
MARY F. C. PRATT (American, contemporary)

Drove to Boston, four hours in wet snow.
Already tired, late flight coming in,
and I'm preaching Christmas Day:
something about snowgeese, maybe,
the way they change the landscape
even after they've flown away—
the way God changed it once,
by making human footprints.
Half the world is here, waiting for planes.
A tall kid in a baseball hat
slouches around, looks at his watch, drinks a Coke.
Passengers from France are surfacing.
The kid spots a first class woman in a suit
crisp and red as a poinsettia,
dances on his toes,
hollers, "Here Mom, over here!"
A thin woman from the back of the plane
stands still as the last tree in the lot,
touches one enameled fingertip to a shadowed eyelid,
shoulders a cheap vinyl bag.
Roaring into the crowd
—did he ride his Harley through this snow?—
a man in a motorcycle jacket
who has not forgotten her.
The lights come on all over town.
The plane from Lisbon lands,

the watchers shift and hum.
A tiny black-eyed boy breaks away,
screaming "POPPY! POPPY!"
runs through the NO UNAUTHORIZED PERSONNEL barrier
as if he's authorized,
throws himself at an old man carrying an umbrella, a paper sack.
Poppy drops his burdens,
raises up the child.
I see ten thousand white geese.
I see starlight on the snow.
The plane from England touches down, taxies in.
The doors open.
When after all these months I see my son
I know that together we have one face,
the face of God,
of someone being born.

―――――

Advent
SUZANNE UNDERWOOD RHODES (American, contemporary)

Through the needle's eye
the rich man came
squeezing through stars
of razor light
that pared his body down to thread.
Gravity crushed his heart's chime
and his breath that breathed out worlds
now flattened as fire between walls.
The impossible slit stripped him,
admitting him
to stitch the human breach.

Mañana (Tomorrow)
LOPE DE VEGA (Spanish, 1562–1635)[6]

Lord, what am I, that, with unceasing care,
  Thou didst seek after me, that thou didst wait,
  Wet with unhealthy dews, before my gate,
  And pass the gloomy nights of winter there?
Oh, strange delusion, that I did not greet
  Thy blest approach! and oh, to Heaven how lost,
  If my ingratitude's unkindly frost
  Has chilled the bleeding wounds upon thy feet!
How oft my guardian angel gently cried,
  "Soul, from thy casement look, and thou shalt see
  How he persists to knock and wait for thee!"
And, oh! how often to that voice of sorrow,
  "To-morrow we will open," I replied,
  And when the morrow came I answered still, "Tomorrow."

———

Nativity of Our Lord and Savior Jesus Christ
CHRISTOPHER SMART (English, 1722–1771)

Where is this stupendous stranger,
  Swains of Solyma,[7] advise,
Lead me to my Master's manger,
  Shew me where my Savior lies?

O Most Mighty! O Most Holy!
  Far beyond the seraph's thought,
Art thou then so mean and lowly
  As unheeded prophets taught?

O the magnitude of meekness!
   Worth from worth immortal sprung;
O the strength of infant weakness,
   If eternal is so young!

If so young and thus eternal,
   Michael tune the shepherd's reed,
Where the scenes are ever vernal,
   And the loves be Love indeed!

See the God blasphem'd and doubted
   In the schools of Greece and Rome;
See the pow'rs of darkness routed,
   Taken at their utmost gloom.

Nature's decorations glisten
   Far above their usual trim;
Birds on box and laurel listen,
   As so near the cherubs' hymn.

Boreas now no longer winters
   On the desolated coast;
Oaks no more are riv'n in splinters
   By the whirlwind and his host.

Spinks and ouzels[8] sing sublimely,
   "We too have a Savior born";
Whiter blossoms burst untimely
   On the blest Mosaic thorn.

God all-bounteous, all-creative,
   Whom no ills from good dissuade,
   Is incarnate, and a native
     Of the very world he made.

———

Nativity

LI-YOUNG LEE (Asian-American, contemporary)

In the dark, a child might ask, *What is the world?*
just to hear his sister
promise, *An unfinished wing of heaven,*
just to hear his brother say,
A house inside a house,
but most of all to hear his mother answer,
One more song, then you go to sleep.

How could anyone in that bed guess
the question finds its beginning
in the answer long growing
inside the one who asked, that restless boy,
the night's darling?

Later, a man lying awake,
he might ask it again,
just to hear the silence
charge him, *This night*
arching over your sleepless wondering,

this night, the near ground
every reaching-out-to overreaches,

just to remind himself
out of what little earth and duration,
out of what immense good-bye,

each must make a safe place of his heart,
before so strange and wild a guest
as God approaches.

———

FROM *A Christmas Carol*

CHARLES DICKENS (English, 1812–1870)

[Editor's note: One of the best-loved Christmas tales of all time hardly needs introduction. The iconic Scrooge plays unwilling host to one strange guest after another, ghosts of his past, present, and future. Here he speaks with the shade of his former partner, Jacob Marley, whose arrival sets off the chain of events that eventually leads to Scrooge's transformation into a man of mercy.]

Mercy!" he said. "Dreadful apparition, why do you trouble me?"

"Man of the worldly mind!" replied the Ghost, "do you believe in me or not?"

"I do," said Scrooge. "I must. But why do spirits walk the earth, and why do they come to me?"

To sit staring at those fixed glazed eyes in silence, for a moment, would play, Scrooge felt, the very deuce with him.

"It is required of every man," the Ghost returned, "that the spirit within him should walk abroad among his fellow-men, and travel far and wide; and, if that spirit goes not forth in life, it is condemned to do so after death. It is doomed to wander through the world—oh, woe is me!—and witness what it cannot share, but might have shared on earth, and turned to happiness!"

Again the specter raised a cry, and shook its chain and wrung its shadowy hands.

"You are fettered," said Scrooge, trembling. "Tell me why?"

"I wear the chain I forged in life," replied the Ghost. "I made it link by link, and yard by yard; I girded it on of my own free-will, and of my own free-will I wore it. Is its pattern strange to *you?*"

Scrooge trembled more and more.

"Or would you know," pursued the Ghost, "the weight and length of the strong coil you bear yourself? It was full as heavy and as long as this, seven Christmas-eves ago. You have labored on it since. It is a ponderous chain!"

Scrooge glanced about him on the floor, in the expectation of finding himself surrounded by some fifty or sixty fathoms of iron cable, but he could see nothing.

"Jacob!" he said imploringly. "Old Jacob Marley, tell me more! Speak comfort to me, Jacob!"

"I have none to give," the Ghost replied. "It comes from other regions, Ebenezer Scrooge, and is conveyed by other ministers, to other kinds of men. Nor can I tell you what I would. A very little more is all permitted to me. I cannot rest, I cannot stay, I cannot linger anywhere. My spirit never walked beyond our counting-house—mark me;—in life my spirit never roved beyond the narrow limits of our money-changing hole; and weary journeys lie before me!"

It was a habit with Scrooge, whenever he became thoughtful, to put his hands in his breeches pockets. Pondering on what the Ghost had said, he did so now, but without lifting up his eyes, or getting off his knees.

"You must have been very slow about it, Jacob," Scrooge observed in a business-like manner, though with humility and deference.

"Slow!" the Ghost repeated.

"Seven years dead," mused Scrooge. "And traveling all the time?"

"The whole time," said the Ghost. "No rest, no peace. Incessant torture of remorse."

"You travel fast?" said Scrooge.

"On the wings of the wind," replied the Ghost.

"You might have got over a great quantity of ground in seven years," said Scrooge.

The Ghost, on hearing this, set up another cry, and clanked its chain so hideously in the dead silence of the night, that the Ward would have been justified in indicting it for a nuisance.

"Oh! captive, bound, and double-ironed," cried the phantom, "not to know that ages of incessant labor, by immortal creatures, for this earth must pass into eternity before the good of which it is susceptible is all developed! Not to know that any Christian spirit working kindly in its little sphere, whatever it may be, will find its mortal life too short for its vast means of usefulness! Not to know that no space of regret can make amends for one life's opportunities misused! Yet such was I! Oh, such was I!"

"But you were always a good man of business, Jacob," faltered Scrooge, who now began to apply this to himself.

"Business!" cried the Ghost, wringing its hands again. "Mankind was my business. The common welfare was my business; charity, mercy, forbearance, and benevolence were, all, my business. The dealings of my trade were but a drop of water in the comprehensive ocean of my business!"

It held up its chain at arm's length, as if that were the cause of all its unavailing grief, and flung it heavily upon the ground again.

"At this time of the rolling year," the specter said, "I suffer most. Why did I walk through crowds of fellow-beings with my eyes turned down, and never raise them to that blessed Star which led the Wise Men to a poor abode? Were there no poor homes to which its light would have conducted *me*?"

Scrooge was very much dismayed to hear the specter going on at this rate, and began to quake exceedingly.

"Hear me!" cried the Ghost. "My time is nearly gone."

"I will," said Scrooge. "But don't be hard upon me! Don't be flowery, Jacob! Pray!"

"How it is that I appear before you in a shape that you can see, I may not tell. I have sat invisible beside you many and many a day."

It was not an agreeable idea. Scrooge shivered, and wiped the perspiration from his brow.

"That is no light part of my penance," pursued the Ghost. "I am here to-night to warn you that you have yet a chance and hope of escaping my fate. A chance and hope of my procuring, Ebenezer."

"You were always a good friend to me," said Scrooge. "Thankee!"

"You will be haunted," resumed the Ghost, "by Three Spirits."

Scrooge's countenance fell almost as low as the Ghost's had done.

"Is that the chance and hope you mentioned, Jacob?" he demanded in a faltering voice.

"It is."

"I—I think I'd rather not," said Scrooge.

"Without their visits," said the Ghost, "you cannot hope to shun the path I tread. Expect the first to-morrow when the bell tolls One."

"Couldn't I take 'em all at once, and have it over, Jacob?" hinted Scrooge.

"Expect the second on the next night at the same hour. The third, upon the next night when the last stroke of Twelve has ceased to vibrate. Look to see me no more; and look that, for your own sake, you remember what has passed between us!"

CHRISTMAS EVE

Between Darkness and Light

OPENING PRAYER

They all were looking for a king
  To slay their foes and lift them high:
Thou cam'st, a little baby thing
  That made a woman cry.
—GEORGE MACDONALD (Scottish, 1824–1905)

SCRIPTURES

PSALM 8 | ISAIAH 9:1–7 | HEBREWS 1:1–12 | LUKE 2:8–20

READINGS

"The Birth of Christ" by ALFRED, LORD TENNYSON
"Nativity" by SCOTT CAIRNS
"Mary" by JOAN RAE MILLS
"Hymn on the Nativity of My Savior" by BEN JONSON
"Shepherd at the Nativity" by TANIA RUNYAN
"Shadow of the Father" by PAUL MARIANI
"The Christmas Story" by WALTER WANGERIN JR.

PERSONAL PRAYER AND REFLECTION

CLOSING PRAYER

Jesu that dost in Mary dwell,
Be in Thy servants' hearts as well,
In the spirit of Thy holiness,
In the fullness of Thy force and stress,
In the very ways that Thy life goes

> And virtues that Thy pattern shows,
>   In the sharing of Thy mysteries;
>   And every power in us that is
> Against thy power put under feet
> In the Holy Ghost the Paraclete
>   To the glory of the Father. Amen.
>
> —GERARD MANLEY HOPKINS (English, 1844–1889)

READINGS

The Birth of Christ

ALFRED, LORD TENNYSON (English, 1809–1892)

The time draws near the birth of Christ;
    The moon is hid—the night is still;
    The Christmas bells from hill to hill
Answer each other in the mist.

Four voices of four hamlets round,
    From far and near, on mead and moor,
    Swell out and fail, as if a door
Were shut between me and the sound.

Each voice four changes on the wind,
    That now dilate and now decrease,
    Peace and good-will, good-will and peace,
Peace and good-will to all mankind.

Rise, happy morn! rise, holy morn!
    Draw forth the cheerful day from night;
    O Father! touch the east, and light
The light that shone when hope was born!

"Nativity" from the poem cycle *Two Icons*
SCOTT CAIRNS (American, contemporary)

As you lean in, you'll surely apprehend
the tiny God is wrapped
in something more than swaddle. The God

is tightly bound within
His blesséd mother's gaze—her face declares
that *she* is rapt by what

she holds, beholds, reclines beholden to.
She cups His perfect head
and kisses Him, that even here the radiant

compass of affection
is announced, that even here our several
histories converge and slip,

just briefly, out of time. Which is much of what
an icon works as well,
and this one offers up a broad array

of separate narratives
whose temporal relations quite miss the point,
or meet there. Regardless,

one blithe shepherd offers music to the flock,
and—just behind him—there
he is again, and sore afraid, attended

by a trembling companion
and addressed by Gabriel. Across the ridge,
three wise men spur three horses

towards a star, and bowing at the icon's
nearest edge, these same three
yet adored the seated One whose mother serves

as throne. Meantime, stumped,
the kindly Abba Joseph ruminates,
receiving consolation

from an attentive dog whose master may
yet prove to be a holy
messenger disguised as fool. Overhead,

the famous star is all
but out of sight by now; yet, even so,
it aims a single ray

directing our slow pilgrims to the core
where all the journeys meet,
appalling crux and hallowed cave and womb,

where crouched among these other
lowing cattle at their trough, our travelers
receive that creature air, and pray.

———

Mary
JOAN RAE MILLS (American, contemporary)

It wasn't that long ago
that he'd spoken these stars
into being
and this woman's life
was just a thought in his mind.
He'd smiled down on her birth
and entered her name in his pages
perhaps with an asterisk
denoting plans too sacred to be spoken
but pondered in his heart.

Now, newborn,
in wide-eyed wonder
he gazes up at his creation.
His hand that hurled the world
holds tight his mother's finger.
Holy light
spills across her face
and she weeps
silent wondering tears
to know she holds the One
who has so long held her.

———

Hymn on the Nativity of My Savior
BEN JONSON (English, 1572–1637)

I sing the birth was born tonight,
The Author both of life and light;
   The angels so did sound it,
And like the ravished shepherds said,
Who saw the light, and were afraid,
   Yet searched, and true they found it.

The Son of God, the eternal King,
That did us all salvation bring,
   And freed the soul from danger;
He whom the whole world could not take,
The Word, which heaven and earth did make,
   Was now laid in a manger.

The Father's wisdom willed it so,
The Son's obedience knew no "No,"
   Both wills were in one stature;

And as that wisdom had decreed,
The Word was now made Flesh indeed,
   And took on Him our nature.

What comfort by Him do we win?
Who made Himself the Prince of sin,
   To make us heirs of glory?
To see this Babe, all innocence,
A Martyr born in our defense,
   Can man forget this story?

———

Shepherd at the Nativity
TANIA RUNYAN (American, contemporary)

Last night I watched another wet lamb
slide into the dark and beheld this same
drowsy beauty: a mother bending toward
her nursing young. New limbs trembling.
Matching rhythms of breath.

The angels told us to praise and adore.
I spend my life trying not to love
such small things. But again and again
I carry my new lambs and name them,
play songs for them on the reed pipe,
bind their broken legs and search for them
in the foothills, until they are sold and worn,
served up, split open on an altar
and I feel my own blood rushing to the edge.

———

Shadow of the Father

PAUL MARIANI (American, contemporary)

How shall I approach you, Joseph, you, the shadow
  of the Father? The stories vary. But who
    were you really? Were you young? Old?

A widower, with children of your own, as the *Proto-
  evangelium* says? I have been to bloody Bethlehem
    and seen the orphaned children there.

A small town, where Palestinian gunmen roamed the Church
  of the Nativity, while Israeli snipers watched
    from the adjoining rooftops. It is a scene not all that

different from Herod's horsemen hunting down a baby,
  though you, dreamer that you were, had already heeded
    the midnight warning and fled with Mary and the baby.

And though they failed to find him, you found him, Joseph,
  and raised him, teaching him your trade, two day laborers
    who must often have queued up, looking for work.

How difficult it must have been, standing in, as every father
  must sometimes feel. Yet where else did your son find
    his courage and outrage against injustice?

How did he become the man he was, if not for you? *"Didn't you know
  I had to be about my father's business?"* Thus the boy, at twelve,
    there in Jerusalem. Words which must have wounded,

though they put the matter in its proper light. After that, you drop
  from history. Saint of happy deaths, was yours a happy death?
    Tradition says it was, logic seems to say it was,

with that good woman and that sweet son there by your side. For
   the past
      two months my wife and her sister have been caring for their
         father, who is dying of cancer. There is the hospital bed,

the potty, the rows of medicine to ease the growing pain. From time
   to time he starts up from his recliner to count his daughters
      and his agèd Irish bride, thinking of a future he no longer

has. When she was little, my wife once told me, she prayed daily
   in the church of St. Benedict to you that she might
      have a daily missal. One day, a man in coveralls

came up to her and—without a word—gave her one with your name
   on it. Oh, she said, her parents would never allow it.
      Put a penny in the poor box, he smiled,

then turned, and disappeared forever. *Who was he?* I asked.
   You know as well as I do who he was, was all she'd say.
      Joseph, be with her now, and with her father, as he faces

the great mystery, as we all must at the end, alone. You seem
   like so many other fathers, who have watched over
      their families, not knowing what the right words were,

but willing to be there for them, up to the very end. Be with them now,
   as you have been for so many others. Give them strength.
      And come, if need be, in a dream, as the angel came to you,

and came to that other Joseph in Egypt so many years before. Be there,
   as once you were in Bethlehem and Nazareth and Queens.
      You, good man, dreamer, the shadow of the Father.

———

The Christmas Story

WALTER WANGERIN JR. (American, contemporary)

And there were shepherds in that same dark country, abiding in the fields, keeping watch over their flocks by night.

And God turned to his angel. And God said, "Gabriel."

And the angel answered, "Yes, Lord?"

And the Lord God said, "Go down. All of the people must know what I am doing. Tired and lonely and scattered and scared, all of the people must hear it. Go, good Gabriel. Go down again. Go tell a few to tell the others, till every child has heard it. Go!"

And so it was that an angel of the Lord appeared to the weary shepherds. Their dark was shattered, for the glory of the Lord shone round about them, and they were sore afraid.

The angel said to them, "Don't be afraid."

But the light was like a hard and holy wind, and the shepherds shielded their faces with their arms.

"Hush," said the angel, "hush," like the west wind. "Shepherds, I bring you good news of great joy, and not only for you but for all of the people. Listen."

So shepherds were squinting and blinking, and shepherds began to listen, but none of them had the courage to talk or to answer a thing.

"For unto you is born this day in the city of David," said the angel, "a Savior, who is Christ the Lord. And this will be a sign for you: you will find the babe wrapped in swaddling clothes and lying in a manger."

Suddenly, the sky itself split open, and like the fall of a thousand stars, the light poured down. There came with the angel a multitude of the heavenly host, praising God and saying,

"Glory to God in the highest,

And on earth, peace—

Peace to the people with whom he is pleased!"

But hush, you shepherds. Hush in your wonder. For the choral singing soon was ended. The host ascended, and the sky was closed again. And then there came a breeze and a marvelous quiet and the simple dark of the night. It was just that, no terror in that then. It was only the night, no deeper gloom than evening. For not all of the light had gone back to heaven. The Light of the World himself stayed down on earth and near you now.

And you can talk now. Try your voices. Try to speak. Ah, God has given you generous voices, shepherds. Speak.

So then, this is what the shepherds said to one another:

"Let us," they said, "go to Bethlehem and see this thing that has happened, which the Lord has made known to us."

So the shepherds got up and ran as fast as they could to the city of Bethlehem, to a particular stable in that city, and in that stable they gazed on one particular baby, lying in a manger.

Then, in that moment, everything was fixed in a lambent, memorial light.

For there was the infant, just waking, just lifting his arms to the air and making sucking motions with his mouth. The holy child was hungry. And there was his mother, lying on straw as lovely as the lily and listening to the noises of her child. "Joseph?" she murmured. And there was Joseph, as sturdy as a barn, just bending toward his Mary. "What?" he whispered.

And the shepherds' eyes were shining for what they saw.

Exactly as though it were morning and not the night, the shepherds went out into the city and began immediately to tell everyone what the angel had said about this child. They left a trail of startled people behind them, as on they went, both glorifying and praising God.

But Mary did not so much as rise that night. She received the baby from Joseph's hands, then placed him down at her breast while she lay on her side on straw. With one arm she cradled the infant against her body. On the other arm, bent at the elbow, she rest her head; and she gazed at her small son sucking. Mary lowered her long, black lashes and watched him and loved him and murmured, "Jesus, Jesus" for the baby's name was Jesus.

"Joseph?" she said without glancing up.

And Joseph said, "What?"

But Mary fell silent and said no more. She was keeping all these things—all that had happened between the darkness and the light—and pondering them in her heart.

CHRISTMAS DAY

This Brief Dawn

OPENING PRAYER

Welcome, all wonders in one sight!
Eternity shut in a span!
 Summer in winter, day in night!
Heaven in earth, and God in man!
 Great little One! whose all-embracing birth
Lifts earth to heaven, stoops heaven to earth.
—RICHARD CRASHAW (English, 1613–1649)

SCRIPTURES

PSALM 113 | ISAIAH 58:8–12 | EPHESIANS 5:8–14 | LUKE 1:68–79

READINGS

"Mary at the Nativity" by TANIA RUNYAN
"Christmas Child" by PAUL WILLIS
"The Adoration of the Infant Jesus" by BENJAMÍN ALIRE SÁENZ
From "The Blessed Virgin Compared to the Air We
Breathe" by GERARD MANLEY HOPKINS
From *A Prayer for Owen Meany* by JOHN IRVING

PERSONAL PRAYER AND REFLECTION

CLOSING PRAYER

Moonless darkness stands between.
Past, the Past, no more be seen!
But the Bethlehem-star may lead me
To the sight of Him Who freed me

From the self that I have been.
Make me pure, Lord: Thou art holy;
Make me meek, Lord: Thou wert lowly;
Now beginning, and alway:
Now begin, on Christmas Day.
——GERARD MANLEY HOPKINS (English, 1844–1889)

READINGS

Mary at the Nativity
TANIA RUNYAN (American, contemporary)

The angel said there would be no end
to his kingdom. So for three hundred days
I carried rivers and cedars and mountains.
Stars spilled in my belly when he turned.

Now I can't stop touching his hands,
the pink pebbles of his knuckles,
the soft wrinkle of flesh
between his forefinger and thumb.
I rub his fingernails as we drift
in and out of sleep. They are small
and smooth, like almond petals.
Forever, I will need nothing but these.

But all night, the visitors crowd
around us. I press his palms to my lips
in silence. They look down in anticipation,
as if they expect him
to spill coins from his hands

or raise a gold scepter
and turn swine into angels.

Isn't this wonder enough
that yesterday he was inside me,
and now he nuzzles next to my heart?
That he wraps his hand around
my finger and holds on?

———

Christmas Child
PAUL WILLIS (American, contemporary)

When you were born, sycamore leaves
were brown and falling. They sifted
through the stable door and laid their hands
upon your cheek. Sunlight bent
through cracks in the wall and found
your lips. It was morning now.
Joseph slept, curled on the straw in a corner.

Your mother offered her breast
to you, the warm milk of humankind,
of kindness. You drank from the spongy
flesh as you could, a long way now
from vinegar, but closer, closer,
closer than the night before.

She cradles you, O Jesus Christ,
born in blood and born to bleed,
for this brief dawn a simple child, searching
the nipple, stirring among the whisper,
the touch, of sycamore.

The Adoration of the Infant Jesus
BENJAMÍN ALIRE SÁENZ (Mexican-American, contemporary)

for Rose

Nostalgia, from
nostos: a return home; and
algos: to be in pain

After Mass this Christmas Day
The people file out. This is
All? Where are the lines?
Expectant crowds? The clamoring
Children waiting to kiss His feet?

I am standing with my mother, my father, my brothers,
And my sisters. I am standing on the tips of my toes
Stretching to see above the heads of those in front.
We crowd into the aisles, shove and push. I smell
Work and perfume; I smell starch and a woman's iron
On the immaculate clothes of those who stand and wait.
We stand together. Here, I am safer—protected in the warmth
Of Spanish. God is so in love with us. I can't wait
To see him. To kiss him, to kiss him. When my lips reach
His feet, he will turn to flesh. I know this. He will
Turn softer than silk, warm as a summer's night,
And he will smile at me. When I reach the holy place,
I stare at the priest who holds the Savior in his arms,
The altar boy who wipes His feet after every kiss.
The priest nods, and when my lips touch the child I have
Waited for, he is warm with the kisses of the people.
I feel the pulse of his blood running through the softness
Of his feet. I know he is breathing. He is alive. He
Is ours. The priest does not know what he holds,
But we who have kissed him know that he is real.

The people here
Do not believe
In lines. Some of us
Do not walk out
The doors. We cannot
Leave this church.
We are few, but we are
Sober as the morning winter
Light. Slowly, one by one,
We kneel before the scene:
A mother, a father, a son;
The sheep, and kings, an angel.
We have known them all our lives.
Mary, the Virgin, the Mother;
Joseph, the Worker, the Father.
The child, the Lover of flesh.
We will love them all our lives.

———

FROM *"The Blessed Virgin Compared to the Air We Breathe"*
GERARD MANLEY HOPKINS (English, 1844–1889)

Wild air, world-mothering air,
Nestling me everywhere,
That each eyelash or hair
Girdles; goes home betwixt
The fleeciest, frailest-flixed
Snowflake; that's fairly mixed
With, riddles, and is rife
In every least thing's life;
This needful, never spent,
And nursing element;

My more than meat and drink,
My meal at every wink;
This air, which, by life's law,
My lung must draw and draw
Now but to breathe its praise,
Minds me in many ways
Of her who not only
Gave God's infinity
Dwindled to infancy
Welcome in womb and breast,
Birth, milk, and all the rest
But mothers each new grace
That does now reach our race—
Mary Immaculate,
Merely a woman, yet
Whose presence, power is
Great as no goddess's
Was deemèd, dreamèd; who
This one work has to do—
Let all God's glory through,
God's glory which would go
Through her and from her flow
Off, and no way but so . . .

———

From *"The Blessed Virgin Compared to the Air We Breathe"* cont.
Gerard Manley Hopkins (English, 1844–1889)

    . . . I say that we are wound
With mercy round and round
As if with air: the same
Is Mary, more by name.

She, wild web, wondrous robe,
Mantles the guilty globe,
Since God has let dispense
Her prayers his providence:
Nay, more than almoner,
The sweet alms' self is her
And men are meant to share
Her life as life does air.
    If I have understood,
She holds high motherhood
Towards all our ghostly good
And plays in grace her part
About man's beating heart,
Laying, like air's fine flood,
The deathdance in his blood;
Yet no part but what will
Be Christ our Savior still.
Of her flesh he took flesh:
He does take fresh and fresh,
Though much the mystery how,
Not flesh but spirit now
And makes, O marvelous!
New Nazareths in us,
Where she shall yet conceive
Him, morning, noon, and eve;
New Bethlems, and he born
There, evening, noon, and morn—
Bethlem or Nazareth,
Men here may draw like breath
More Christ and baffle death;
Who, born so, comes to be
New self and nobler me
In each one and each one

More makes, when all is done,
Both God's and Mary's Son . . .

. . . So God was God of old:
A mother came to mould
Those limbs like ours which are
What must make our daystar
Much dearer to mankind;
Whose glory bare would blind
Or less would win man's mind.
Through her we may see him
Made sweeter, not made dim,
And her hand leaves his light
Sifted to suit our sight.
Be thou then, O thou dear
Mother, my atmosphere;
My happier world, wherein
To wend and meet no sin;
Above me, round me lie
Fronting my froward eye
With sweet and scarless sky;
Stir in my ears, speak there
Of God's love, O live air,
Of patience, penance, prayer:
World-mothering air, air wild,
Wound with thee, in thee isled,
Fold home, fast fold thy child.

———

FROM *A Prayer for Owen Meany*

JOHN IRVING (American, contemporary)

[Editor's note: If Jesus had been an American boy in the 1950s—
the son of working-class parents, small in stature, sharp, and with a
"wrecked voice" (Irving has him speak in all caps)—he might have
been something like Owen Meany. One Christmas Owen convinces
the local pastor (Rev. Wiggin) and his wife, Barb, that he should play
the baby Jesus in the church pageant, doted upon by the socially inept
Mary Beth Baird (as Mary) and Owen's own friend Johnny Wheel-
wright (as Joseph)—our narrator. Here, amidst endless negotiations
between Owen and Barb Wiggin—who deeply regrets allowing
Owen to play Jesus—they rehearse the big event.]

Mary Beth Baird foresaw a larger problem. Since the reading
from Luke concluded by observing that "Mary kept all these
things, pondering them in her heart"—and surely the "things" that
Mary so kept and pondered were far more matterful than these
trivial gifts—shouldn't she *do* something to demonstrate to the audience what a strain on her poor heart it was to do such monumental
keeping and pondering?

"What?" Barb Wiggin said.

"WHAT SHE MEANS IS, SHOULDN'T SHE *ACT OUT*
HOW A PERSON *PONDERS* SOMETHING," Owen said. Mary
Beth Baird was so pleased that Owen had clarified her concerns
that she appeared on the verge of hugging or kissing him, but Barb
Wiggin moved quickly between them, leaving the controls of the
"pillar of light" unattended; eerily, the light scanned our little assem-
bly with a will of its own—appearing to settle on the Holy Mother.

There was a respectful silence while we pondered what possible
thing Mary Beth Baird *could* do to demonstrate how hard her heart
was working; it was clear to most of us that Mary Beth would be
satisfied only if she could express her adoration of the Christ Child
physically.

"I could kiss him," Mary Beth said softly. "I could just bow down and kiss him—on the forehead, I mean."

"Well, yes, you could try that, Mary Beth," the rector said cautiously.

"Let's see how it looks," Barb Wiggin said doubtfully.

"NO," Owen said. "NO KISSING."

"Why not, Owen," Barb Wiggin asked playfully. She thought an opportunity to tease him was presenting itself, and she was quick to pounce on it.

"THIS IS A VERY HOLY MOMENT," Owen said slowly.

"Indeed, it is," the rector said.

"VERY HOLY," Owen said. "SACRED," he added.

"Just on the forehead," Mary Beth said.

"Let's see how it looks. Let's just try it, Owen," Barb Wiggin said.

"NO," Owen said. "IF MARY IS SUPPOSED TO BE *PONDERING*—'IN HER HEART'—THAT I AM CHRIST THE LORD, THE ACTUAL SON OF GOD . . . A *SAVIOR*, REMEMBER THAT . . . DO YOU THINK SHE'D JUST KISS ME LIKE SOME ORDINARY MOTHER KISSING HER ORDINARY BABY? THIS IS NOT THE ONLY TIME THAT MARY *KEEPS THINGS IN HER HEART*. DON'T YOU REMEMBER WHEN THEY GO TO JERUSALEM FOR PASSOVER AND JESUS GOES TO THE TEMPLE AND TALKS TO THE TEACHERS, AND JOSEPH AND MARY ARE WORRIED ABOUT HIM BECAUSE THEY CAN'T FIND HIM—THEY'RE LOOKING ALL OVER FOR HIM—AND HE TELLS THEM, WHAT ARE YOU WORRIED ABOUT, WHAT ARE YOU LOOKING FOR ME FOR, 'DID YOU NOT KNOW THAT I MUST BE IN MY FATHER'S HOUSE?' HE MEANS THE TEMPLE. REMEMBER THAT? WELL, MARY KEEPS THAT IN HER HEART, TOO."

"But shouldn't I *do* something, Owen?" Mary Beth asked. "What should I do?"

"YOU KEEP THINGS IN YOUR HEART!" Owen told her.

"She should do nothing?" the Rev. Mr. Wiggin asked Owen. The rector, like one of the teachers in the temple, appeared "amazed." That is how the teachers in the temple are described—in their response to the Boy Jesus: "All who heard him were amazed at his understanding and his answers."

"Do you mean she should do nothing, Owen?" the rector repeated. "Or that she should do something less, or more, than kissing?"

"MORE," Owen said. Mary Beth Baird trembled; she would do anything he required. "TRY BOWING," Owen suggested.

"Bowing?" Barb Wiggin said, with distaste.

Mary Beth Baird dropped to her knees and lowered her head; she was an awkward girl, and this sudden movement caused her to lose her balance. She assumed a three-point position, finally—on her knees, with her forehead resting on the mountain of hay, the top of her head pressing against Owen's hip.

Owen raised his hand over her, to bless her; in a most detached manner, he lightly touched her hair—then his hand hovered above her head, as if he meant to shield her eyes from the intensity of the "pillar of light." Perhaps, if only for this gesture, Owen had wanted his arms free.

The shepherds and kings were riveted to this demonstration of what Mary pondered in her heart; the cows did not move. Even the hind parts of the donkeys, who could not see the Holy Mother bowing to the Baby Jesus—or anything at all—appeared to sense that the moment was reverential; they ceased their swaying, and the donkey's tails hung straight and still. Barb Wiggin had stopped breathing, with her mouth open, and the rector wore the numbed expression of one struck silly with awe. And I, Joseph—I did nothing, I was just the witness. God knows how long Mary Beth Baird would have buried her head in the hay, for no doubt she was ecstatic to have the top of her head in contact with the Christ Child's hip. We might have maintained our positions in this tableau for eternity—we might have made crèche history, a pageant frozen in rehearsal, each of us injected with the very magic we sought to represent: Nativity forever.

But the choirmaster, whose eyesight was failing, assumed he had missed the cue for the final carol, which the choir sang with special gusto.

> Hark! the her-ald an-gels sing, "Glory to the new-born King;
> Peace on earth, and mer-cy mild, God and sin-ners rec-on-ciled!"
> Joy-ful, all ye na-tions, rise, Join the tri-umph of the skies;
> With the an-gel-ic host pro-claim, "Christ is born in Beth-le-hem!"
> Hark! the her-ald an-gels sing, "Glor-y to the new-born King!"

Mary Beth Baird's head shot up at the first "Hark!" Her hair was wild and flecked with hay; she jumped to her feet as if the little Prince of Peace had ordered her out of his nest. The donkeys swayed again, the cows—their horns falling about their heads—moved a little, and the kings and shepherds regained their usual lack of composure. The rector, whose appearance suggested that of a former immortal rudely returned to the rules of the earth, found that he could speak again. "That was perfect, I thought," he said. "That was *marvelous*, really."

"Shouldn't we run through it one more time?" Barb Wiggin asked, while the choir continued to herald the birth of "the ever-lasting Lord."

"NO," said the Prince of Peace. "I THINK WE'VE GOT IT RIGHT."

FIRST SUNDAY AFTER CHRISTMAS

Saints and Sinners

OPENING PRAYER

Hear us, O hear us Lord; to Thee
A sinner is more music, when he prays,
Than spheres, or angels' praises be,
In panegyric alleluias,
Hear us, for till Thou hear us, Lord
We know not what to say.
—JOHN DONNE (English, 1572–1631)

SCRIPTURES

PSALM 112 | ECCLESIASTES 5:1–7 | JAMES 1:2–16 | LUKE 2:22–40

READINGS

"Joseph at the Nativity" by TANIA RUNYAN
"Advent" by ENUMA OKORO
"Nature" by GEORGE HERBERT
"Into Solitude" by ANNA KAMIEŃSKA
From *The Brothers Karamazov* by FYODOR DOSTOEVSKY

PERSONAL PRAYER AND REFLECTION

CLOSING PRAYER

Thine ear to our sighs, tears, thoughts gives voice and word.
O Thou who Satan heard'st in Job's sick day,
Hear Thyself now, for Thou in us dost pray.
—JOHN DONNE (English, 1572–1631)

❦

READINGS

Joseph at the Nativity
TANIA RUNYAN (American, contemporary)

Of any birth, I thought this
would be a clean one,
like pulling white linen
from a loom.

But when I return to the cave,
Mary throws her cloak
over the bloody straw and cries.
I know she wants me to leave.

There he lies, stomach rising
and falling, a shriveled pod
that does nothing but stare
at the edge of the feeding trough
with dark, unsteady eyes.

Is he God enough
to know that I am poor,
that we had no time
for a midwife, that swine ate
from his bed this morning?

If the angel was right, he knows.
He knows that Mary's swell
embarrassed me, that I was jealous
of her secret skyward smiles,
that now I want to run into these hills
and never come back.

Peace, peace, I've heard in my dreams.
This child will make you right.

But I can only stand here,
not a husband, not a father,
my hands hanging dumbly
at my sides. Do I touch him,
this child who is mine
and not mine? Do I enter
the kingdom of blood and stars?

———

Advent

ENUMA OKORO (Nigerian-American, contemporary)

I want to find my place
amongst the people of Advent
but I can't quite decide who I am.
I want to be pregnant with God
but it takes such a toll on the body.
I have given birth to things before
And labor is hard and untimely.

I want to welcome angels and say yes,
to anything.
but if I saw an angel I would hold him
hostage and send a ransom note of questions
demanding answers, to God.

I want to cheer blessings from the sidelines
with a belly growing with prophecies,
and have friends and strangers take hope.
Because God has a season
for those whose seasons have passed.

I want to put my trust in dreams
and in the words of the ones I love,
to believe that God is as close as
the one who would share my bed.

But mostly I want a break from being
the one who mostly falls silent
in the presence of all that's holy,
who loses her words in disbelief,
terrified by claims of joy and gladness,
unable to believe that prayers are answered.

———

Nature
GEORGE HERBERT (English, 1593–1633)

Full of rebellion, I would die,
    Or fight, or travel, or deny
That thou hast ought to do with me.
            O tame my heart;
        It is thy highest art
To captivate strong holds to thee.

If thou shalt let this venom lurk,
And in suggestions fume and work,
My soul will turn to bubbles straight,
            And thence by kind
        Vanish into a wind,
Making thy workmanship deceit.

O smooth my rugged heart, and there
Engrave thy rev'rend law and fear;
Or make a new one, since the old
            Is sapless grown,

And a much fitter stone
To hide my dust, than thee to hold.

———

Into Solitude
ANNA KAMIEŃSKA (Polish, 1920–1986)

We descend into solitude step by step
further and further down stanzas of verses
into depths never expected
determined to live without poor substitutes
in a cruel and impossible purity
there at the very bottom to regain
all those who huddle
at the gate of this wide-open emptiness
grandmothers aunts and uncles already forgotten
strangers who once crossed a courtyard
someone out of work who knocked on the window
someone passed by on a footbridge
the dead the living it doesn't matter
the beautiful boy who stood below the pulpit
looking like an angel almost an angel
and the one who hit me on the forehead with a stone
where a mark still remains
and the washerwoman who reappeared at our home like Kronos
and went away bent under the weight of the laundry basket
the wagon-driver with whom I danced at the harvest festival
and Someone else was there a carpenter or a woodworker
who placed a hand on my forehead
and said Don't be afraid
with me no one is lonely

———

From *The Brothers Karamazov*

FYODOR DOSTOEVSKY (Russian, 1821–1881)

[Editor's note: Among the brothers Karamazov is the youngest, Alyosha, who has joined the local monastery headed by an elder, Father Zossima. In one scene, the elder is visited by a variety of pilgrims who seek his help, counsel, or healing, including this well-to-do lady with her young daughter, Lise. Here the lady expresses her spiritual questions and struggles.]

I suffer . . . from lack of faith."

"Lack of faith in God?"

"Oh, no, no! I dare not even think of that. But the future life—it is such an enigma! And no one, no one can solve it. Listen! You are a healer, you are deeply versed in the human soul, and of course I dare not expect you to believe me entirely, but I assure you on my word of honor that I am not speaking lightly now. The thought of the life beyond the grave distracts me to anguish, to terror. And I don't know to whom to appeal, and have not dared to all my life. And now I am so bold as to ask you. Oh, God! What will you think of me now?"

She clasped her hands.

"Don't distress yourself about my opinion of you," said the elder. "I quite believe in the sincerity of your suffering."

"Oh, how thankful I am to you! You see, I shut my eyes and ask myself if every one has faith, where did it come from? And then they do say that it all comes from terror at the menacing phenomena of nature, and that none of it's real. And I say to myself, 'What if I've been believing all my life, and when I come to die there's nothing but the burdocks growing on my grave?' as I read in some author. It's awful! How—how can I get back my faith? But I only believed when I was a little child, mechanically, without thinking of anything. How, how is one to prove it? I have come now to lay my soul before you and to ask you about it. If I let this chance slip, no one all my life will answer me. How can I prove it? How can I convince myself? Oh, how unhappy I am! I stand and look about me and see that scarcely any one else cares; no one troubles his head about it, and I'm the only one who can't stand it. It's deadly—deadly!"

"No doubt. But there's no proving it, though you can be convinced of it."

"How?"

"By the experience of active love. Strive to love your neighbor actively and indefatigably. In as far as you advance in love you will grow surer of the reality of God and of the immortality of your soul. If you attain to perfect self-forgetfulness in the love of your neighbor, then you will believe without doubt, and no doubt can possibly enter your soul. This has been tried. This is certain."

"In active love? There's another question—and such a question! You see, I so love humanity that—would you believe it?—I often dream of forsaking all that I have, leaving Lise, and becoming a sister of mercy. I close my eyes and think and dream, and at that moment I feel full of strength to overcome all obstacles. No wounds, no festering sores could at that moment frighten me. I would bind them up and wash them with my own hands. I would nurse the afflicted. I would be ready to kiss such wounds."

"It is much, and well that your mind is full of such dreams and not others. Sometime, unawares, you may do a good deed in reality."

"Yes. But could I endure such a life for long?" the lady went on fervently, almost frantically. "That's the chief question—that's my most agonizing question. I shut my eyes and ask myself, 'Would you persevere long on that path? And if the patient whose wounds you are washing did not meet you with gratitude, but worried you with his whims, without valuing or remarking your charitable services, began abusing you and rudely commanding you, and complaining to the superior authorities of you (which often happens when people are in great suffering)—what then? Would you persevere in your love, or not?' And do you know, I came with horror to the conclusion that, if anything could dissipate my love to humanity, it would be ingratitude. In short, I am a hired servant, I expect my payment at once—that is, praise, and the repayment of love with love. Otherwise I am incapable of loving any one."

She was in a very paroxysm of self-castigation, and, concluding, she looked with defiant resolution at the elder.

"It's just the same story as a doctor once told me," observed the elder. "He was a man getting on in years, and undoubtedly clever. He spoke as frankly as you, though in jest, in bitter jest. 'I love humanity,' he said, 'but I wonder at myself. The more I love humanity in general, the less I love man in particular. In my dreams,' he said, 'I have often come to making enthusiastic schemes for the service of humanity, and perhaps I might actually have faced crucifixion if it had been suddenly necessary; and yet I am incapable of living in the same room with any one for two days together, as I know by experience. As soon as any one is near me, his personality disturbs my self-complacency and restricts my freedom. In twenty-four hours I begin to hate the best of men: one because he's too long over his dinner; another because he has a cold and keeps on blowing his nose. I become hostile to people the moment they come close to me. But it has always happened that the more I detest men individually the more ardent becomes my love for humanity.'"

"But what's to be done? What can one do in such a case? Must one despair?"

"No. It is enough that you are distressed at it. Do what you can, and it will be reckoned unto you. Much is done already in you since you can so deeply and sincerely know yourself. If you have been talking to me so sincerely, simply to gain approbation for your frankness, as you did from me just now, then of course you will not attain to anything in the achievement of real love; it will all get no further than dreams, and your whole life will slip away like a phantom. In that case you will naturally cease to think of the future life too, and will of yourself grow calmer after a fashion in the end."

"You have crushed me! Only now, as you speak, I understand that I was really only seeking your approbation for my sincerity when I told you I could not endure ingratitude. You have revealed me to myself. You have seen through me and explained me to myself!"

"Are you speaking the truth? Well, now, after such a confession, I believe that you are sincere and good at heart. If you do not attain happiness, always remember that you are on the right road, and try not to leave it. Above all, avoid falsehood, every kind of falsehood, especially falseness to yourself. Watch over your own deceitfulness and look into it every hour, every minute. Avoid being scornful, both to others and to yourself. What seems to you bad within you will grow purer from the very fact of your observing it in yourself. Avoid fear, too, though fear is only the consequence of every sort of falsehood. Never be frightened at your own faint-heartedness in attaining love. Don't be frightened overmuch even at your evil actions. I am sorry I can say nothing more consoling to you, for love in action is a harsh and dreadful thing compared with love in dreams. Love in dreams is greedy for immediate action, rapidly performed and in the sight of all. Men will even give their lives if only the ordeal does not last long but is soon over, with all looking on and applauding as though on the stage. But active love is labor and fortitude, and for some people too, perhaps, a complete science. But I predict that just when you see with horror that in spite of all your efforts you are getting farther from your goal instead of nearer to it—at that very moment I predict that you will reach it and behold clearly the miraculous power of the Lord who has been all the time loving and mysteriously guiding you. Forgive me for not being able to stay longer with you. They are waiting for me. Good-bye."

The lady was weeping.

SECOND SUNDAY AFTER CHRISTMAS

Stunned Back to Belief

OPENING PRAYER

Up, up, my soul, on wings of praise,
No other service know;
In holy strains the love express
That fires the heart below.
—Adapted from the poetry of SYNESIUS (Greek, AD 375–430)

SCRIPTURES

PSALM 96 | ISAIAH 6:1–8 | REVELATION 4:1–11 | LUKE 2:41–51

READINGS

"O That With Yonder Sacred Throng" by MARCI JOHNSON
"The Seraph and Poet" by ELIZABETH BARRETT BROWNING
"Staying Power" by JEANNE MURRAY WALKER
"Stunned Back to Belief While the Mezzo Sang 'He Shall Feed His
Flock'" by MARY F. C. PRATT
"Made Flesh" by LUCI SHAW
"Ring Out Wild Bells" by ALFRED, LORD TENNYSON
From *Godric* by FREDERICK BUECHNER

PERSONAL PRAYER AND REFLECTION

CLOSING PRAYER

Burn, burn, my soul, and ever be
With holy ardor fired,
And, strongly armed with firm resolve,
Be evermore inspired.
—Adapted from the poetry of SYNESIUS (Greek, AD 375–430)

READINGS

O That With Yonder Sacred Throng
MARCI JOHNSON (American, contemporary)

The things of this world do not seem
to be going according to plan.

For one thing, the altar's on fire.
The pastor hasn't noticed, thinks

the audience is unusually moved
by his words his sharp suit the way

his thick hair waves at a part
so straight the Israelites could pass

through to the Promised Land with
out detour. A man in back has gone

for the fire extinguisher while
we like sheep look to one another

to gauge reaction. Shall we finish
the final hymn? Remark on the too

obvious symbolism? No, let's throw
our bodies on the flames Old Testament

style like a people uncivilized by bulletins
and keyboards and cupped ceiling

lights but living in the raw wind, the
hunger, the sand in our upturned faces.

The Seraph and Poet

ELIZABETH BARRETT BROWNING (English, 1806–1861)

The seraph sings before the manifest
God-One, and in the burning of the Seven,
And with the full life of consummate Heaven
Heaving beneath him like a mother's breast
Warm with her first-born's slumber in that nest.
The poet sings upon the earth grave-riven,
Before the naughty world, soon self-forgiven
For wronging him,—and in the darkness press'd
From his own soul by worldly weights. Even so,
Sing, seraph with the glory! heaven is high;
Sing, poet with the sorrow! earth is low:
The universe's inward voices cry
"Amen" to either song of joy and woe:
Sing, seraph,—poet,—sing on equally!

———

Staying Power

JEANNE MURRAY WALKER (American, contemporary)

> *In appreciation of Maxim Gorky at the International
> Convention of Atheists. 1929*

Like Gorky, I sometimes follow my doubts
outside and question the metal sky,
longing to have the fight settled, thinking
I can't go on like this, and finally I say

all right, it is improbable, all right, there
is no God. And then as if I'm focusing
a magnifying glass on dry leaves, God blazes up.
It's the attention, maybe, to what isn't

there that makes the notion flare like
a forest fire until I have to spend the afternoon
dragging the hose to put it out. Even
on an ordinary day when a friend calls,

tells me they've found melanoma,
complains that the hospital is cold, I say God.
God, I say as my heart turns inside out.
Pick up any language by the scruff of its neck,

wipe its face, set it down on the lawn,
and I bet it will toddle right into the godfire
again, which—though they say it doesn't
exist—can send you straight to the burn unit.

Oh, we have only so many words to think with.
Say God's not fire, say anything, say God's
a phone, maybe. You know you didn't order a phone,
but there it is. It rings. You don't know who it could be.

You don't want to talk, so you pull out
the plug. It rings. You smash it with a hammer
till it bleeds springs and coils and clobbered up
metal bits. It rings again. You pick it up

and a voice you love whispers hello.

———

Stunned Back to Belief While the Mezzo Sang "He Shall Feed His Flock"

MARY F. C. PRATT (American, contemporary)

For the mezzo, Wendy Hoffman-Farrell

. . . I always used to believe he would,
but lately, with life wandering out of control—
beasts, sharp edges everywhere—
I have not been so sure.
Concentrating on my part—
the crazy alto timing in "He shall purify,"
the slippery bits in "Unto us"—
I was forgetting to listen.
But then her voice.
Not like light—
not clear, star-studded, disturbing,
the dangerous sky of a wild and wakeful night—
but close and warm and dark,
the safe dark when everything that can harm is asleep,
the comforting dark when you have been gathered up
and peek out at the puzzling world
from the folds of his robes,
the happiness of his encircling arms.

Made Flesh

LUCI SHAW (naturalized U.S. citizen, contemporary)

After
the bright beam of hot annunciation
fused heaven with dark earth
his searing sharply focused light

went out for a while
eclipsed in amniotic gloom:
his cool immensity of splendor
his universal grace
small-folded in a warm dim
female space—
the Word stern-sentenced
to be nine months dumb—
infinity walled in a womb
until the next enormity—
the Mighty, after submission
to a woman's pains
helpless on a barn-bare floor
first-tasting bitter death.

Now
I in him surrender
to the crush and cry of birth.
Because eternity
was closeted in time
he is my open door
to forever.
From his imprisonment my freedoms grow,
find wings.
Part of his body, I transcend this flesh.
From his sweet silence my mouth sings.
Out of his dark I glow.
My life, as his,
slips through death's mesh,
time's bars,
joins hands with heaven,
speaks with stars.

"Ring Out Wild Bells" FROM "In Memoriam A.H.H."

ALFRED, LORD TENNYSON (English, 1809–1892)

Ring out, wild bells, to the wild sky,
　　The flying cloud, the frosty light:
　　The year is dying in the night;
Ring out, wild bells, and let him die.

Ring out the old, ring in the new,
　　Ring, happy bells, across the snow:
　　The year is going, let him go;
Ring out the false, ring in the true.

Ring out the grief that saps the mind
　　For those that here we see no more;
　　Ring out the feud of rich and poor,
Ring in redress to all mankind.

Ring out a slowly dying cause,
　　And ancient forms of party strife;
　　Ring in the nobler modes of life,
With sweeter manners, purer laws.

Ring out the want, the care, the sin,
　　The faithless coldness of the times;
　　Ring out, ring out my mournful rhymes
But ring the fuller minstrel in.

Ring out false pride in place and blood,
　　The civic slander and the spite;
　　Ring in the love of truth and right,
Ring in the common love of good.

Ring out old shapes of foul disease;
　　Ring out the narrowing lust of gold;
　　Ring out the thousand wars of old,
Ring in the thousand years of peace.

Ring in the valiant man and free,
  The larger heart, the kindlier hand;
  Ring out the darkness of the land,
Ring in the Christ that is to be.

———

From *Godric*

FREDERICK BUECHNER (American, contemporary)

[Editor's note: Elderly Saint Godric, summoned from his hermitage at the River Wear, continues on his pilgrimage to Durham Cathedral for Christmas. Assisted by his fellow monks, Perkin and Reginald, he is greeted as a celebrity by Bishop Pudsey.]

Flanked by monks, the Bishop waits on the cathedral steps, his mitre white with snow. Reginald and Perkin help me up to him, and when I kneel to kiss his ring, it takes all three to hoist me back upon my feet. Hugh Pudsey's barely old enough to sprout a beard, and yet a bishop and a mighty lord as well.

"It's I should kneel to you," he says.

I say, "Pray don't, my lord, or we'll spend Christmas bobbing up and down like turnips at the boil."

The monks have brought a chair with poles to carry me. I haven't been inside since Bishop Flambard's time. The aisles are vaulted now. The nave is done. Thick Norman columns stout enough to hold the welkin up support the high, dim vaulting of the roof. The columns have been carved around with deep-cut lines like garlands, serpents, crooked vines, each different from the rest. Behind the altar there's a shrine to shelter Cuthbert's bones they carted here, with many stoppings over many years along the way, from Lindisfarne.

Even the flames of many candles can't light up this awesome dark, nor all the gathered throng of priests and monks and lords and common folk fill up this emptiness. The hooded monks chant psalms as we wend slowly down, but all their voices raised at once are but the rustle of the wind through trees, the call of owls, in this vast wood of stone. The towns the Conqueror razed when he came harrying the north, the crops he burned, the beasts he felled, the Saxon folk he slew, all haunt these Norman shadows. The silence is the sum of all their voices stilled. As long as these stones stand and this great roof keeps out the rain, Durham's cathedral will be dark with death.

They set my chair down near the altar. Reginald rejoins his fellow monks and takes a choir stall. Perkin stands by me. He whispers in my ear, "If you grow weary, tug my sleeve. I'll cart you to a tavern on my back, and there we'll raise a cup to Christ."

I set my finger to my lips and scowl, but I am glad he's there. His face is all aglow with candlelight. His eyes are young and Christmas-bright. The Christmas mass begins.

"*Lux fulgebit hodie!*"[9] they sing. "The Lord is born to us! *Wonderful* shall be his name, and *God*, the *Prince of Peace*, the *Father of the world to come!*" And even as their monkish voices dip and soar like doves, I see with my heart's eye the steaming dung of beasts, their cloudy breath, the cloddish shepherds at the door. I see the holy mother gazing down, and there among them, in the straw, the fresh-born king.

An easy thing it is to love a babe. A babe asks nothing, never chides. A babe is fair to see. A babe is hope for better things to come. All this and more. But babes grow into men at last. That's where it turns a bitter brew. "He hath no form or comeliness," Isaiah says. "No beauty that we should desire him. A man of sorrows we despise." Christ minds us to be good, to feed his sheep, take up our cross and follow him with Hell's hot fires if we fail. All this and more our Savior bids when he becomes a man, and to a man we say him nay. Thus when the Bishop tenders me with his own hands Christ's flesh and blood, I slobber them with tears.

"Bear up, old man," says Perkin in my ear.

But there's more here than can be borne. The gorgeous robes of priests. The altar all aflame. The clouds of incense rich and sharp. And in the midst old Godric, keeping Christmas, blubbers like a child.

EPIPHANY

All of Us Magi

OPENING PRAYER

That thou art nowhere to be found, agree
Wise men, whose eyes are but for surfaces;
Men with eyes opened by the second birth,
To whom the seen, husk of the unseen is,
Descry thee soul of everything on earth.
Who know thy ends, thy means and motions see;
Eyes made for glory soon discover thee.
—GEORGE MACDONALD (Scottish, 1824–1905)

SCRIPTURES
PSALM 19 | MICAH 5:2–5 | ROMANS 15:7–13 | MATTHEW 2:1–12

READINGS
"Nativity" by JOHN DONNE
"The Christ-child Lay on Mary's Lap" by G. K. CHESTERTON
"Star Song" by ELIZABETH B. ROONEY
"The Starlight Night" by GERARD MANLEY HOPKINS
From "The Other Wise Man" by HENRY VAN DYKE

PERSONAL PRAYER AND REFLECTION

CLOSING PRAYER
Oh, happiest who before Thine altar wait,
  With pure hands ever holding up on high
The guiding Star of all who seek Thy gate,
  The undying lamp of heavenly Poesy.
—JOHN KEBLE (English, 1792–1866)

✺

READINGS

Nativity
JOHN DONNE (English, 1572–1631)

Immensity cloister'd in thy dear womb,
Now leaves His well-beloved imprisonment.
There He hath made Himself to His intent
Weak enough, now into our world to come.
But O! for thee, for Him, hath th' inn no room?
Yet lay Him in this stall, and from th' orient,
Stars, and wise men will travel to prevent
Th' effect of Herod's jealous general doom.
See'st thou, my soul, with thy faith's eye, how He
Which fills all place, yet none holds Him, doth lie?
Was not His pity towards thee wondrous high,
That would have need to be pitied by thee?
Kiss Him, and with Him into Egypt go,
With His kind mother, who partakes thy woe.

———

The Christ-child Lay on Mary's Lap
G. K. CHESTERTON (English, 1874–1936)

The Christ-child lay on Mary's lap,
His hair was like a light.
(O weary, weary were the world,
But here is all aright.)

order of Magi to meet with him regarding some strange portents in the sky. Among his guests are his venerable mentor Abgarus and the skeptical Tigranes. Artaban begins the meeting by affirming his fellow Magi's quest for knowledge, of which the study of the stars is highest; but then asserts that the quest must end not in darkness and conflict but in light and truth—according to one of the Magi's own ancient prophecies. His mentor, Abgarus, approves what he says, but then Artaban takes the conversation in an unexpected direction.]

M y father, I have kept this prophecy in the secret place of my soul. Religion without a great hope would be like an altar without a living fire. And now the flame has burned more brightly, and by the light of it I have read other words which also have come from the fountain of Truth, and speak yet more clearly of the rising of the Victorious One in his brightness."

He drew from the breast of his tunic two small rolls of fine linen, with writing upon them, and unfolded them carefully upon his knee.

"In the years that are lost in the past, long before our fathers came into the land of Babylon, there were wise men in Chaldea, from whom the first of the Magi learned the secret of the heavens. And of these Balaam the son of Beor was one of the mightiest. Hear the words of his prophecy: 'There shall come a star out of Jacob, and a scepter shall arise out of Israel.'"

The lips of Tigranes drew downward with contempt, as he said:

"Judah was a captive by the waters of Babylon, and the sons of Jacob were in bondage to our kings. The tribes of Israel are scattered through the mountains like lost sheep, and from the remnant that dwells in Judea under the yoke of Rome neither star nor scepter shall arise."

"And yet," answered Artaban, "it was the Hebrew Daniel, the mighty searcher of dreams, the counselor of kings, the wise Belteshazzar, who was most honored and beloved of our great King

Cyrus. A prophet of sure things and a reader of the thoughts of God, Daniel proved himself to our people. And these are the words that he wrote." (Artaban read from the second roll:)

"'Know, therefore, and understand that from the going forth of the commandment to restore Jerusalem, unto the Anointed One, the Prince, the time shall be seven and threescore and two weeks.'"

"But, my son," said Abgarus, doubtfully, "these are mystical numbers. Who can interpret them, or who can find the key that shall unlock their meaning?"

Artaban answered: "It has been shown to me and to my three companions among the Magi—Caspar, Melchior, and Balthazar. We have searched the ancient tablets of Chaldea and computed the time. It falls in this year. We have studied the sky, and in the spring of the year we saw two of the greatest stars draw near together in the sign of the Fish, which is the house of the Hebrews. We also saw a new star there, which shone for one night and then vanished. Now again the two great planets are meeting. This night is their conjunction. My three brothers are watching at the ancient Temple of the Seven Spheres, at Borsippa, in Babylonia, and I am watching here. If the star shines again, they will wait ten days for me at the temple, and then we will set out together for Jerusalem, to see and worship the promised one who shall be born King of Israel. I believe the sign will come. I have made ready for the journey. I have sold my house and my possessions, and bought these three jewels—a sapphire, a ruby, and a pearl—to carry them as tribute to the King. And I ask you to go with me on the pilgrimage, that we may have joy together in finding the Prince who is worthy to be served."

While he was speaking he thrust his hand into the inmost fold of his girdle and drew out three great gems—one blue as a fragment of the night sky, one redder than a ray of sunrise, and one as pure as the peak of a snow mountain at twilight—and laid them on the out-spread linen scrolls before him.

But his friends looked on with strange and alien eyes. A veil of doubt and mistrust came over their faces, like a fog creeping up from the marshes to hide the hills. They glanced at each other with looks of wonder and pity, as those who have listened to incredible sayings, the story of a wild vision, or the proposal of an impossible enterprise.

At last Tigranes said: "Artaban, this is a vain dream. It comes from too much looking upon the stars and the cherishing of lofty thoughts. It would be wiser to spend the time in gathering money for the new fire-temple at Chala. No king will ever rise from the broken race of Israel, and no end will ever come to the eternal strife of light and darkness. He who looks for it is a chaser of shadows. Farewell."

And another said: "Artaban, I have no knowledge of these things, and my office as guardian of the royal treasure binds me here. The quest is not for me. But if thou must follow it, fare thee well."

And another said: "In my house there sleeps a new bride, and I cannot leave her nor take her with me on this strange journey. This quest is not for me. But may thy steps be prospered wherever thou goest. So, farewell."

And another said: "I am ill and unfit for hardship, but there is a man among my servants whom I will send with thee when thou goest, to bring me word how thou farest."

But Abgarus, the oldest and the one who loved Artaban the best, lingered after the others had gone, and said, gravely: "My son, it may be that the light of truth is in this sign that has appeared in the skies, and then it will surely lead to the Prince and the mighty brightness. Or it may be that it is only a shadow of the light, as Tigranes has said, and then he who follows it will have only a long pilgrimage and an empty search. But it is better to follow even the shadow of the best than to remain content with the worst. And those who would see wonderful things must often be ready to travel alone. I am too old for this journey, but my heart shall be a companion of the pilgrimage day and night, and I shall know the end of thy quest. Go in peace."

So one by one they went out of the azure chamber with its silver stars, and Artaban was left in solitude.

He gathered up the jewels and replaced them in his girdle. For a long time he stood and watched the flame that flickered and sank upon the altar. Then he crossed the hall, lifted the heavy curtain, and passed out between the dull red pillars of porphyry to the terrace on the roof.

The shiver that thrills through the earth ere she rouses from her night sleep had already begun, and the cool wind that heralds the daybreak was drawing downward from the lofty, snow-traced ravines of Mount Orontes. Birds, half awakened, crept and chirped among the rustling leaves, and the smell of ripened grapes came in brief wafts from the arbors.

Far over the eastern plain a white mist stretched like a lake. But where the distant peak of Zagros serrated the western horizon the sky was clear. Jupiter and Saturn rolled together like drops of lambent flame about to blend in one.

As Artaban watched them, behold, an azure spark was born out of the darkness beneath, rounding itself with purple splendors to a crimson sphere, and spiring upward through rays of saffron and orange into a point of white radiance. Tiny and infinitely remote, yet perfect in every part, it pulsated in the enormous vault as if the three jewels in the Magian's breast had mingled and been transformed into a living heart of light.

He bowed his head. He covered his brow with his hands.

"It is the sign," he said. "The King is coming, and I will go to meet him."

The Holy Innocents

OPENING PRAYER

O Lord, my praying hear;
    Lord, let my cry come to thine ear.
Hide not thy face away,
    But haste, and answer me,
In this my most, most miserable day,
    Wherein I pray and cry to thee.
—MARY SIDNEY HERBERT, Countess of Pembroke (English,
1561–1621)

SCRIPTURES

PSALM 10 | JEREMIAH 31:15–20 | REVELATION 12:1–17 |
MATTHEW 2:13–18

READINGS

"Childhood Stories" by GRAŽINA BIELOUSOVA
"Day VI: The War" by EUGENE PETERSON
From "The Other Wise Man" by HENRY VAN DYKE
From *Mr. Ives' Christmas* by OSCAR HIJUELOS
"Solace" by DICK ALLEN

PERSONAL PRAYER AND REFLECTION

CLOSING PRAYER

But what is this if I
    In the mid way should fall and die?
My God, to thee I pray,

> Who canst my prayer give.
> Turn not to night the noontide of my day,
>   Since endless thou dost ageless live.
> —MARY SIDNEY HERBERT, Countess of Pembroke (English,
> 1561–1621)

READINGS

Childhood Stories
GRAŽINA BIELOUSOVA (Lithuanian, contemporary)

I will never forget the story
I was never supposed to know—
Nor was my mom, who as a child
Overheard some distant relative of hers
After a couple shots of vodka
In a large family get-together brag
About his war-time heroic deeds
Of cleansing the country from the Jews:
"I'd take a kid and throw him up in the air
And shoot him. By the time
He hit the ground, he was already dead . . . "
I can see him grab the baby from the crib,
A helpless bundle, unsuspecting of such evil,
See him perform his act of murder
In the eyes of the screaming mother . . .

No, I will never forget the story
I heard as a child, long ago,
When my mom amidst her never-ending chores
Instead of fairy tales would talk to me

About life, the family and the war,
About her father, who in a Nazi train,
Bound to where no one had come back from,
By accident discovered a loose board
And before anyone had the wit
To realize what that could mean,
He pushed himself outside
And quickly hid under the train,
Firmly pressing his body against the rails . . .

Who knows how many horror seconds
He had to count before the dusk fell
On the station and he could steal away.

How could I ever forget the story
I heard by my grandmother told
About the times when during the war
Betrayed by her own cousin
She awoke one night with someone
Thumping on the door.
(And they almost started to believe
They had survived the worst!)
The overcrowded cattle wagons
With every turn over of heavy wheels
Crushed her dreams to study
And maybe one day to teach,
Her teenagerish romance—
Oh that blue eyed curly chap
With whom she loved to dance!—
Her very life that was worth nothing,
One among the agony of thousands others
Buried under the cover of Siberian snow.
She says it was so unimaginably cold
That even icicles hanging down

Their log cabin's ceiling
Would never melt.

I will always remember the story
I heard about my grandpa told
How famished and frozen stiff
They, ragged soldiers, in the dead of winter,
Came across a good-hearted peasant
Who shared the best he had with them—
Jars of honey, honey dripping from aluminum spoons,
Luscious and sweet beyond what their tongues,
Unaccustomed to such luxury, could lick . . .
They gorged themselves on the amber sweet—
Who knows when someone else will offer anything to eat?—
Until all of them were poison-sick
With honey oozing from the pores of their skin,
And vomiting the precious treat . . .
Afterwards, I heard, my grandpa
Would not even touch the sweets.

I will never forget these stories—
How could I?
How could anyone even fall asleep,
When against the dark screen of night
All these stories come alive
And slowly flow before the eyes?
History does not ask names,
Preferences and point-of-views
And the most unlikely find themselves
Saying things and acting in ways
That otherwise they would have never dared.
But where, O God, in history do I look for you?
No one telling their stories
Gave you credit, nobody blamed.

I don't know if in the midst of horror
They remembered how to pray.

———

"Day VI: The War" FROM the poem cycle
The Twelve Days of Christmas
EUGENE PETERSON (American, contemporary)

> *And the dragon stood before the woman who was about to*
> *bear a child, that he might devour her child . . . Now war*
> *arose in heaven. Revelation 12:4, 7*

This birth's a signal for war. Lovers fight,
Friends fall out. Merry toasts from flagons
Of punch are swallowed in the maw of dragons.
Will mother and baby survive this devil night?

> I've done my share of fighting in the traffic:
> Kitchen quarrels, playground fisticuffs:
> Every cherub choir has its share of toughs,
> And then one day I learned the fight was cosmic.

Truce: I lay down arms; my arms fill up
With gifts: wild and tame, real and stuffed

> Lions. Lambs play, oxen low,
> The infant fathers festive force. One crow

Croaks defiance into the shalom whiteness,
Empty, satanic bluster against the brightness.

———

HENRY VAN DYKE (American, 1852–1933)

[Editor's note: The fourth Wise Man makes his way across the desert, lagging behind his peers, and arrives at Bethlehem after they have already left. Wandering through the village, he has the following encounter.]

From the open door of a low stone cottage he heard the sound of a woman's voice singing softly. He entered and found a young mother hushing her baby to rest. She told him of the strangers from the far East who had appeared in the village three days ago, and how they said that a star had guided them to the place where Joseph of Nazareth was lodging with his wife and her new-born child, and how they had paid reverence to the child and given him many rich gifts.

"But the travelers disappeared again," she continued, "as suddenly as they had come. We were afraid at the strangeness of their visit. We could not understand it. The man of Nazareth took the babe and his mother and fled away that same night secretly, and it was whispered that they were going far away to Egypt. Ever since, there has been a spell upon the village; something evil hangs over it. They say that the Roman soldiers are coming from Jerusalem to force a new tax from us, and the men have driven the flocks and herds far back among the hills, and hidden themselves to escape it."

Artaban listened to her gentle, timid speech, and the child in her arms looked up in his face and smiled, stretching out its rosy hands to grasp at the winged circle of gold on his breast. His heart warmed to the touch. It seemed like a greeting of love and trust to one who had journeyed long in loneliness and perplexity, fighting with his own doubts and fears, and following a light that was veiled in clouds.

"Might not this child have been the promised Prince?" he asked within himself, as he touched its soft cheek. "Kings have been born ere now in lowlier houses than this, and the favorite of the stars may rise even from a cottage. But it has not seemed good to the God of wisdom to reward my search so soon and so easily. The one whom I seek has gone before me; and now I must follow the King to Egypt."

The young mother laid the babe in its cradle, and rose to minister to the wants of the strange guest that fate had brought into her house. She set food before him, the plain fare of peasants, but willingly offered, and therefore full of refreshment for the soul as well as for the body. Artaban accepted it gratefully; and, as he ate, the child fell into a happy slumber, and murmured sweetly in its dreams, and a great peace filled the quiet room.

But suddenly there came the noise of a wild confusion and uproar in the streets of the village, a shrieking and wailing of women's voices, a clangor of brazen trumpets and a clashing of swords, and a desperate cry: "The soldiers! the soldiers of Herod! They are killing our children."

The young mother's face grew white with terror. She clasped her child to her bosom, and crouched motionless in the darkest corner of the room, covering him with the folds of her robe, lest he should wake and cry.

But Artaban went quickly and stood in the doorway of the house. His broad shoulders filled the portal from side to side, and the peak of his white cap all but touched the lintel.

The soldiers came hurrying down the street with bloody hands and dripping swords. At the sight of the stranger in his imposing dress they hesitated with surprise. The captain of the band approached the threshold to thrust him aside. But Artaban did not stir. His face was as calm as though he were watching the stars, and in his eyes there burned that steady radiance before which even the half-tamed hunting leopard shrinks, and the fierce blood-hound pauses in his leap. He held the soldier silently for an instant, and then said in a low voice:

"I am all alone in this place, and I am waiting to give this jewel to the prudent captain who will leave me in peace."

He showed the ruby, glistening in the hollow of his hand like a great drop of blood.

The captain was amazed at the splendor of the gem. The pupils of his eyes expanded with desire, and the hard lines of greed wrinkled around his lips. He stretched out his hand and took the ruby.

"March on!" he cried to his men, "there is no child here. The house is still."

———

FROM *Mr. Ives' Christmas*

OSCAR HIJUELOS (Cuban-American, 1951–2013)

[Editor's note: Pulitzer Prize–winning author Oscar Hijuelos, who died unexpectedly while this anthology was being compiled, told this quiet tale of one good man's shattering grief. For Mr. Ives, orphaned as a child and raised by a kind adoptive father, 1950s New York was always magical at Christmastime. But then came a Christmas Eve in the 1960s when life for the advertising illustrator and his wife, Annie—parents of teenagers Caroline and Robert—changed forever.]

They were in one of those states that come from having had enough to drink but not enough to ward off an early hangover, and as they made their way from the 116th Street station toward Claremont, Ives began to suffer from a headache and was thinking that he would have a nice glass of scotch at home and take a couple of aspirins. Maybe they would order takeout from the Chinese joint on 124th, or go to the local bar, Malloy's, whose big sign he himself had designed and painted, where they had good tap beer and hamburgers rated among the best in the city, Ives in the mood for its unsavory atmosphere every so often. But as Ives and Annie passed 120th Street and were approaching their building, they could see people milling about in front of their stoop—dozens of their neighbors, among them Ramirez and his son, who came solemnly toward them, Ramirez' face a mask of grief. Two police cars were parked in front. The first thing Ives thought was that something had happened to Caroline: she was getting strong-headed lately and might have gone off to the park by herself, which he had warned her about a hundred times, but soon he saw her on the stoop, her head buried against Carmen Ramirez' arms. And then he saw Mr. Ramirez' stony face, eyes wide open: with Ives' forearm in his grip, he squeezed it more tightly than it had ever been squeezed before, and he said: "*Hermano.*"[10] And shortly, as Annie stood atop the steps with her daughter, shopping bags by her side, Ives found himself walking between two plainclothes police officers. Then, leaving Caroline with Mrs. Ramirez, Annie got into the back beside her husband.

As the automobile pulled away from the curb, another green-and-white police car followed. Ives and Annie did not say a word and just watched the streets and lights flashing by as they made their way along Tiemann to 123rd, and then uptown again. A train pulled into the elevated station and his wife, nestling her head against his shoulder, sighed. He noticed that in a first-floor window on Broadway a family had put up a lovely display of the Holy Mother posed in a Christmas setting, with a wreath of red and pink and light blue electric lights blinking crazily around her, and that she was flanked by two oversized electric candles, which gave off a tremendous pink light, the kind of gaudy but pleasing display one generally found in the poorer parts of the city.

Then the cop behind the wheel offered each a cigarette, and Ives said rather matter-of-factly, "No thanks, but that brand is one of my company's biggest advertisers."

In the back of that police car, he remembered a four-color ad he had drawn one Christmas, about 1954–1955, for a toy company: in it, a young sleepy-eyed boy, newly awakened on Christmas morning, stands before a richly decorated tree, gasping with delight over an electric train set, an illustration he had based on his son. The boy looked just like Robert, and Ives could see him crawling around the floor of their old apartment on Fiftieth Street and exploring the lowest boughs of the Christmas tree, strands of tinsel, lights and ornaments glowing like majestic stars above him; his son reaching up, his son's fine lips slightly parted, heavy-lidded eyes wide.

And then Ives blinked and found himself standing on the sidewalk beside his wife, across the street from the Church of the Ascension. On the pavement, just by his feet, was a large piece of canvas, and under it a body, stretched out. Then the officer lifted off the canvas and shined a flashlight onto the face to reveal the shocked and bewildered expression of his son.

———

Solace

Dick Allen (American, contemporary)

Newtown, CT
December 2012

There are the fields we'll walk across
In the snow lightly falling.
     In the snow lightly falling,
There are the fields we'll walk across.

There are the houses we'll walk toward
In the snow lightly falling.
     In the snow lightly falling,
There are the houses we'll walk toward.

There are the faces we once kissed
In the snow lightly falling.
     In the snow lightly falling,
There are the faces we once kissed.

Incredible how we laughed and cried
In the snow lightly falling.
          In the snow lightly falling,
Incredible how we laughed and cried.

Incredible how we'll meet again
In the snow lightly falling.
          In the snow lightly falling,
Incredible how we'll meet again.

No small hand will go unheld
In the snow lightly falling
          In the snow lightly falling,
No small hand will go unheld.

No voice once heard is ever lost
In the snow lightly falling.
          In the snow lightly falling,
No voice once heard is ever lost.

EPIPHANY WEEK 2

Faith of a Child

Thou canst not have forgotten all
That it feels like to be small:
And Thou know'st I cannot pray
To Thee in my father's way—
When Thou wast so little, say,
Couldst Thou talk Thy Father's way?—
—FRANCIS THOMPSON (English, 1859–1907)

SCRIPTURES
PSALM 131 | ISAIAH 11:1–9 | 1 JOHN 3:1–3 | MARK 10:13–16

READINGS
"A Christmas Carol" by CHRISTINA ROSSETTI
"It is as if infancy were the whole of incarnation" by LUCI SHAW
"Temple" by JOHN DONNE
"After Three Days" by LEWIS CARROLL
From *The Gifts of the Christ Child* by GEORGE MACDONALD

PERSONAL PRAYER AND REFLECTION

CLOSING PRAYER
So, a little Child, come down
And hear a child's tongue like Thy own;
Take me by the hand and walk,
And listen to my baby-talk.
—FRANCIS THOMPSON (English, 1859–1907)

READINGS

A Christmas Carol
CHRISTINA ROSSETTI (English, 1830–1894)

In the bleak midwinter, frosty wind made moan,
Earth stood hard as iron, water like a stone;
Snow had fallen, snow on snow, snow on snow,
In the bleak midwinter, long ago.

Our God, Heaven cannot hold Him, nor earth sustain;
Heaven and earth shall flee away when He comes to reign.
In the bleak midwinter a stable place sufficed
The Lord God Almighty, Jesus Christ.

Enough for Him, whom cherubim, worship night and day,
Breastful of milk, and a mangerful of hay;
Enough for Him, whom angels fall before,
The ox and ass and camel which adore.

Angels and archangels may have gathered there,
Cherubim and seraphim thronged the air;
But His mother only, in her maiden bliss,
Worshipped the beloved with a kiss.

What can I give Him, poor as I am?
If I were a shepherd, I would bring a lamb;
If I were a Wise Man, I would do my part;
Yet what I can I give Him: give my heart.

It is as if infancy were the whole of incarnation
LUCI SHAW (naturalized U.S. Citizen, contemporary)

One time of the year
the new-born child
is everywhere,
planted in madonnas' arms
hay mows, stables,
in palaces or farms,
or quaintly, under snowed gables,
gothic angular or baroque plump,
naked or elaborately swathed,
encircled by Della Robbia wreaths,
garnished with whimsical
partridges and pears,
drummers and drums,
lit by oversize stars,
partnered with lambs,
peace doves, sugar plums,
bells, plastic camels in sets of three
as if these were what we need
for eternity.

But Jesus the Man is not to be seen.
We are too wary, these days,
of beards and sandalled feet.

Yet if we celebrate, let it be
that He
has invaded our lives with purpose,
striding over our picturesque traditions,
our shallow sentiment,
overturning our cash registers,
wielding His peace like a sword,

rescuing us into reality,
demanding much more
than the milk and the softness
and the mother warmth
of the baby in the storefront crèche,
(only the Man would ask
all, of each of us)
reaching out
always, urgently, with strong
effective love
(only the Man would give
His life and live
again for love of us).

Oh come, let us adore Him—
Christ—*the Lord*.

———

Temple
JOHN DONNE (English, 1572–1631)

With His kind mother, who partakes thy woe,
Joseph, turn back; see where your child doth sit,
Blowing, yea blowing out those sparks of wit,
Which Himself on the doctors did bestow.
The Word but lately could not speak, and lo!
It suddenly speaks wonders; whence comes it,
That all which was, and all which should be writ,
A shallow seeming child should deeply know?
His Godhead was not soul to His manhood,
Nor had time mellow'd Him to this ripeness;
But as for one which hath a long task, 'tis good,
With the sun to begin His business,

He in His age's morning thus began,
By miracles exceeding power of man.

———

After Three Days
LEWIS CARROLL (English, 1832–1898)

I stood within the gate
Of a great temple, 'mid the living stream
Of worshipers that thronged its regal state
Fair-pictured in my dream.

Jewels and gold were there;
And floors of marble lent a crystal sheen
To body forth, as in a lower air,
The wonders of the scene.

Such wild and lavish grace
Had whispers in it of a coming doom;
As richest flowers lie strown about the face
Of her that waits the tomb.

The wisest of the land
Had gathered there, three solemn trysting-days,
For high debate: men stood on either hand
To listen and to gaze.

The aged brows were bent,
Bent to a frown, half thought, and half annoy,
That all their stores of subtlest argument
Were baffled by a boy.

In each averted face
I marked but scorn and loathing, till mine eyes
Fell upon one that stirred not in his place,
Tranced in a dumb surprise.

Surely within his mind
Strange thoughts are born, until he doubts the lore
Of those old men, blind leaders of the blind,
    Whose kingdom is no more.

    Surely he sees afar
A day of death the stormy future brings;
The crimson setting of the herald-star
    That led the Eastern kings.

    Thus, as a sunless deep
Mirrors the shining heights that crown the bay,
So did my soul create anew in sleep
    The picture seen by day.

    Gazers came and went—
A restless hum of voices marked the spot—
In varying shades of critic discontent
    Prating they knew not what.

    "Where is the comely limb,
The form attuned in every perfect part,
The beauty that we should desire in him?"
    Ah! Fools and slow of heart!

    Look into those deep eyes,
Deep as the grave, and strong with love divine;
Those tender, pure, and fathomless mysteries,
    That seem to pierce through thine.

    Look into those deep eyes,
Stirred to unrest by breath of coming strife,
Until a longing in thy soul arise
    That this indeed were life:

    That thou couldst find Him there,
Bend at His sacred feet thy willing knee,

And from thy heart pour out the passionate prayer
    "Lord, let me follow Thee!"

But see the crowd divide:
Mother and sire have found their lost one now:
The gentle voice, that fain would seem to chide
    Whispers "Son, why hast thou"—

In tone of sad amaze—
"Thus dealt with us, that art our dearest thing?
Behold, thy sire and I, three weary days,
    Have sought thee sorrowing."

And I had stayed to hear
The loving words "How is it that ye sought?"—
But that the sudden lark, with matins clear,
    Severed the links of thought.

Then over all there fell
Shadow and silence; and my dream was fled,
As fade the phantoms of a wizard's cell
    When the dark charm is said.

Yet, in the gathering light,
I lay with half-shut eyes that would not wake,
Lovingly clinging to the skirts of night
    For that sweet vision's sake.

————

FROM *The Gifts of the Christ Child*
GEORGE MACDONALD (Scottish, 1824–1905)

[Editor's note: Victorian minister George MacDonald, himself a man
of childlike faith, created a number of memorable child characters,
including Phosy (or Sophy, for *wisdom*) in this short story. At church

one Sunday in Advent she takes the notion literally that Jesus is born every Christmas. Meanwhile, her stepmother, who is pregnant, goes into early labor on Christmas Eve.]

It was the morning of Christmas Day, and little Phosy knew it in every cranny of her soul. She was not of those who had been up all night, and now she was awake, early and wide, and the moment she awoke she was speculating: He was coming to-day—how would he come? Where should she find the baby Jesus? And when would he come? In the morning, or the afternoon, or in the evening? Could such a grief be in store for her as that he would not appear until night, when she would be again in bed? But she would not sleep till all hope was gone. Would everybody be gathered to meet him, or would he show himself to one after another, each alone? Then her turn would be last, and oh, if he would come to the nursery! But perhaps he would not appear to her at all!—for was she not one whom the Lord did not care to chasten?

Expectation grew and wrought in her until she could lie in bed no longer. Alice was fast asleep. It must be early, but whether it was yet light or not she could not tell for the curtains. Anyhow she would get up and dress, and then she would be ready for Jesus whenever he should come. True, she was not able to dress herself very well, but he would know, and would not mind. She made all the haste she could, consistently with taking pains, and was soon attired after a fashion.

She crept out of the room and down the stair. The house was very still. What if Jesus should come and find nobody awake? Would he go again and give them no presents? She couldn't expect any herself—but might he not let her take theirs for the rest? Perhaps she ought to wake them all, but she dared not without being sure.

On the last landing above the first floor, she saw, by the low gaslight at the end of the corridor, an unknown figure pass the foot of the stair: could she have anything to do with the marvel of the day? The woman looked up, and Phosy dropped the question. Yet she might be a charwoman, whose assistance the expected advent rendered necessary. When she reached the bottom of the stair she saw her disappearing in her step-mother's room. That she did not like. It was the one room into which she could not go. But, as the house was so still, she would search everywhere else, and if she did not find him, would then sit down in the hall and wait for him.

The room next the foot of the stair, and opposite her step-mother's, was the spare room, with which she associated ideas of state and grandeur: where better could she begin than at the guest-chamber?—There!—Could it be? Yes!—Through the chink of the scarce-closed door she saw light. Either he was already there or there they were expecting him. From that moment she felt as if lifted out of the body. Far exalted above all dread, she peeped modestly in, and then entered. Beyond the foot of the bed, a candle stood on a little low table, but nobody was to be seen. There was a stool near the table: she would sit on it by the candle, and wait for him. But ere she reached it, she caught sight of something upon the bed that drew her thither. She stood entranced.—Could it be?—It might be. Perhaps he had left it there while he went into her mamma's room with something for her.—The loveliest of dolls ever imagined! She drew nearer. The light was low, and the shadows were many: she could not be sure what it was. But when she had gone close up to it, she concluded with certainty that it was in very truth a doll—perhaps intended for her—but beyond doubt the most exquisite of dolls. She dragged a chair to the bed, got up, pushed her little arms softly under it, and drawing it gently to her, slid down with it. When she felt her feet firm on the floor, filled with the solemn composure of holy awe she carried the gift of the child Jesus to the candle, that she might the better admire its beauty and know its preciousness.

But the light had no sooner fallen upon it than a strange unde-finable doubt awoke within her. Whatever it was, it was the very essence of loveliness—the tiny darling with its alabaster face, and its delicately modeled hands and fingers! A long night-gown covered all the rest.—Was it possible?—Could it be?—Yes, indeed! it must be—it could be nothing else than a real baby! What a goose she had been! Of course it was baby Jesus himself!—for was not this his very own Christmas Day on which he was always born?—If she had felt awe of his gift before, what a grandeur of adoring love, what a divine dignity possessed her, holding in her arms the very child himself! One shudder of bliss passed through her, and in an agony of possession she clasped the baby to her great heart—then at once became still with the satisfaction of eternity, with the peace of God. She sat down on the stool, near the little table, with her back to the candle, that its rays should not fall on the eyes of the sleeping Jesus and wake him: there she sat, lost in the very majesty of bliss, at once the mother and the slave of the Lord Jesus.

EPIPHANY WEEK 3

Costly Gifts

OPENING PRAYER

O Thou, who keep'st the Key of Love,
  Open Thy fount, eternal Dove,
    And overflow this heart of mine,
  Enlarging as it fills with Thee,
  Till in one blaze of charity
Care and remorse are lost, like motes in light divine . . .
—JOHN KEBLE (English, 1792–1866)

SCRIPTURES

PSALM 103 | ISAIAH 53:1–6 | PHILIPPIANS 2:1–11 | LUKE 7:36–50

READINGS

"The Forest Primeval" by PAUL WILLIS
"A quintina of crosses" by CHAD WALSH
"The First Christmas Tree" by EUGENE FIELD

PERSONAL PRAYER AND REFLECTION

CLOSING PRAYER

Thou know'st our service sad and hard,
  Thou know'st us fond and frail;
Win us to be loved and spared
  When all the world shall fail.
—JOHN KEBLE (English, 1792–1866)

✠

READINGS

The Forest Primeval
PAUL WILLIS (American, contemporary)

I am five years old. It is a lamentable
week—or two weeks—after Christmas in Anaheim.
All the way around the block there are
Christmas trees at mute attention on the curb.
They are stripped of lights and stars and angels,
and lean against the garbage cans with only a trace
or two of tinsel, tawdry in the morning light.

These trees are lonely, I decide. They need
to be brought together somewhere to commiserate,
to regain a semblance of miracle. Somewhere
like my backyard. One by one, on a rescue mission,
I drag them down the sidewalk and around our house
and plant them one against the other, a thick
entangling of grateful boughs. All afternoon

I crawl inside their fragrant shade, touching open
pockets of pitch and feeling needles rain down
softly in my hair. The trees are happy to be so close.
They recall what it was like to flourish in peace, to offer
their presence, young as they are, an ancient grove.
It is a delight to have them here, in my backyard, here
where we will grow together for many years,
where I will always be the gift beneath these trees.

———

A quintina of crosses
CHAD WALSH (American, 1914–1991)

Beyond, beneath, within, wherever blood,
If there were blood, flows with the pulse of love,
Where God's circle and all orbits cross,
Through the black space of death to baby life
Came God, planting the secret genes of God.

By the permission of a maiden's love,
Love came upon the seeds of words, broke blood,
And howled into the Palestine of life,
A baby roiled by memories of God.
Sometimes he smiled, sometimes the child was cross.

Often at night he dreamed a dream of God
And was the dream he dreamed. Often across
The lily fields he raged and lived their life,
And heaven's poison festered in his blood,
Loosing the passion of unthinkable love.

But mostly, though, he lived a prentice's life
Until a singing in the surge of blood,
Making a chorus of the genes of God,
Flailed him into the tempest of a love
That lashed the North Star and the Southern Cross.

His neighbors smelled an alien in his blood,
A secret enemy and double life;
He was a mutant on an obscene cross
Outraging decency with naked love.
He stripped the last rags from a proper God.

The life of God must blood this cross for love.

The First Christmas Tree

EUGENE FIELD (American, 1850–1895)

Once upon a time the forest was in a great commotion. Early in the evening the wise old cedars had shaken their heads ominously and predicted strange things. They had lived in the forest many, many years; but never had they seen such marvelous sights as were to be seen now in the sky, and upon the hills, and in the distant village.

"Pray tell us what you see," pleaded a little vine; "we who are not as tall as you can behold none of these wonderful things. Describe them to us, that we may enjoy them with you."

"I am filled with such amazement," said one of the cedars, "that I can hardly speak. The whole sky seems to be aflame, and the stars appear to be dancing among the clouds; angels walk down from heaven to the earth, and enter the village or talk with the shepherds upon the hills."

The vine listened in mute astonishment. Such things never before had happened. The vine trembled with excitement. Its nearest neighbor was a tiny tree, so small it scarcely ever was noticed; yet it was a very beautiful little tree, and the vines and ferns and mosses and other humble residents of the forest loved it dearly.

"How I should like to see the angels!" sighed the little tree, "and how I should like to see the stars dancing among the clouds! It must be very beautiful."

As the vine and the little tree talked of these things, the cedars watched with increasing interest the wonderful scenes over and beyond the confines of the forest. Presently they thought they heard music, and they were not mistaken, for soon the whole air was full of the sweetest harmonies ever heard upon earth.

"What beautiful music!" cried the little tree. "I wonder whence it comes."

"The angels are singing," said a cedar; "for none but angels could make such sweet music."

"But the stars are singing, too," said another cedar; "yes, and the shepherds on the hills join in the song, and what a strangely glorious song it is!"

The trees listened to the singing, but they did not understand its meaning: it seemed to be an anthem, and it was of a Child that had been born; but further than this they did not understand. The strange and glorious song continued all the night; and all that night the angels walked to and fro, and the shepherd-folk talked with the angels, and the stars danced and caroled in high heaven. And it was nearly morning when the cedars cried out, "They are coming to the forest! the angels are coming to the forest!" And, surely enough, this was true. The vine and the little tree were very terrified, and they begged their older and stronger neighbors to protect them from harm. But the cedars were too busy with their own fears to pay any heed to the faint pleadings of the humble vine and the little tree. The angels came into the forest, singing the same glorious anthem about the Child, and the stars sang in chorus with them, until every part of the woods rang with echoes of that wondrous song. There was nothing in the appearance of this angel host to inspire fear; they were clad all in white, and there were crowns upon their fair heads, and golden harps in their hands; love, hope, charity, compassion, and joy beamed from their beautiful faces, and their presence seemed to fill the forest with a divine peace. The angels came through the forest to where the little tree stood, and gathering around it, they touched it with their hands, and kissed its little branches, and sang even more sweetly than before. And their song was about the Child, the Child, the Child that had been born. Then the stars came down from the skies and danced and hung upon the branches of the tree, and they, too, sang that song,—the song of the Child. And all the other trees and the vines and the ferns and the mosses beheld in wonder;

nor could they understand why all these things were being done, and why this exceeding honor should be shown the little tree.

When the morning came the angels left the forest,—all but one angel, who remained behind and lingered near the little tree. Then a cedar asked: "Why do you tarry with us, holy angel?" And the angel answered: "I stay to guard this little tree, for it is sacred, and no harm shall come to it."

The little tree felt quite relieved by this assurance, and it held up its head more confidently than ever before. And how it thrived and grew, and waxed in strength and beauty! The cedars said they never had seen the like. The sun seemed to lavish its choicest rays upon the little tree, heaven dropped its sweetest dew upon it, and the winds never came to the forest that they did not forget their rude manners and linger to kiss the little tree and sing it their prettiest songs. No danger ever menaced it, no harm threatened; for the angel never slept,—through the day and through the night the angel watched the little tree and protected it from all evil. Oftentimes the trees talked with the angel; but of course they understood little of what he said, for he spoke always of the Child who was to become the Master; and always when thus he talked, he caressed the little tree, and stroked its branches and leaves, and moistened them with his tears. It all was so very strange that none in the forest could understand.

So the years passed, the angel watching his blooming charge. Sometimes the beasts strayed toward the little tree and threatened to devour its tender foliage; sometimes the woodman came with his axe, intent upon hewing down the straight and comely thing; sometimes the hot, consuming breath of drought swept from the south, and sought to blight the forest and all its verdure: the angel kept them from the little tree. Serene and beautiful it grew, until now it was no longer a little tree, but the pride and glory of the forest.

One day the tree heard some one coming through the forest. Hitherto the angel had hastened to its side when men approached; but now the angel strode away and stood under the cedars yonder.

"Dear angel," cried the tree, "can you not hear the footsteps of some one approaching? Why do you leave me?"

"Have no fear," said the angel; "for He who comes is the Master."

The Master came to the tree and beheld it. He placed His hands upon its smooth trunk and branches, and the tree was thrilled with a strange and glorious delight. Then He stooped and kissed the tree, and then He turned and went away.

Many times after that the Master came to the forest, and when He came it always was to where the tree stood. Many times He rested beneath the tree and enjoyed the shade of its foliage, and listened to the music of the wind as it swept through the rustling leaves. Many times He slept there, and the tree watched over Him, and the forest was still, and all its voices were hushed. And the angel hovered near like a faithful sentinel.

Ever and anon men came with the Master to the forest, and sat with Him in the shade of the tree, and talked with Him of matters which the tree never could understand; only it heard that the talk was of love and charity and gentleness, and it saw that the Master was beloved and venerated by the others. It heard them tell of the Master's goodness and humility,—how He had healed the sick and raised the dead and bestowed inestimable blessings wherever He walked. And the tree loved the Master for His beauty and His goodness; and when He came to the forest it was full of joy, but when He came not it was sad. And the other trees of the forest joined in its happiness and its sorrow, for they, too, loved the Master. And the angel always hovered near.

The Master came one night alone into the forest, and His face was pale with anguish and wet with tears, and He fell upon His knees and prayed. The tree heard Him, and all the forest was still, as if it were standing in the presence of death. And when the morning came, lo! the angel had gone.

Then there was a great confusion in the forest. There was a sound of rude voices, and a clashing of swords and staves. Strange men appeared, uttering loud oaths and cruel threats, and the tree was filled with terror. It called aloud for the angel, but the angel came not.

"Alas," cried the vine, "they have come to destroy the tree, the pride and glory of the forest!"

The forest was sorely agitated, but it was in vain. The strange men plied their axes with cruel vigor, and the tree was hewn to the ground. Its beautiful branches were cut away and cast aside, and its soft, thick foliage was strewn to the tenderer mercies of the winds.

"They are killing me!" cried the tree; "why is not the angel here to protect me?"

But no one heard the piteous cry,—none but the other trees of the forest; and they wept, and the little vine wept too.

Then the cruel men dragged the despoiled and hewn tree from the forest, and the forest saw that beauteous thing no more.

But the night wind that swept down from the City of the Great King that night to ruffle the bosom of distant Galilee, tarried in the forest awhile to say that it had seen that day a cross upraised on Calvary,—the tree on which was stretched the body of the dying Master.

EPIPHANY WEEK 4

The Soul in Suffering

Lord Jesus, think on me,
Nor let me go astray;
Through darkness and perplexity
Point Thou the heav'nly way.
—Adapted from the poetry of SYNESIUS (Greek, AD 375–430)

SCRIPTURES

PSALM 88 | JOB 3 | ROMANS 5:1–11 | JOHN 11:17–37

READINGS

"Cemetery" by BENJAMÍN ALIRE SÁENZ
"The Stricken" by PAUL WILLIS
"What Would I Give?" by CHRISTINA ROSSETTI
"Psalm 55" by MARY SIDNEY HERBERT
"Tears" by ELIZABETH BARRETT BROWNING
From *The Gifts of the Christ Child* by GEORGE MACDONALD

PERSONAL PRAYER AND REFLECTION

CLOSING PRAYER

I take my heart in my hand—
  I shall not die, but live—
Before Thy face I stand;
  I, for Thou callest such:
All that I have I bring,
  All that I am I give,

Smile Thou and I shall sing,
But shall not question much.
—CHRISTINA ROSSETTI (English, 1830–1894)

READINGS

Cemetery

BENJAMÍN ALIRE SÁENZ (Mexican-American, contemporary)

I walk these grassless grounds
Cracked, withering in weeds. My eyes move
From one monument to the next: a star
For the hour of their births, a cross
For the hour of their deaths. Grave after
Grave, row after crooked row like fields
Of rotting corn.
                                My eyes fall
On words: *Para mi querido hijo*, a mother's
Final letter to her war-dead son. The foreigner
Has found a place, died for a flag that knows only
How to wave *adiós* in English. A broken angel,
Wingless, protects the grave of an infant
Whose name the wind has stolen.
                                                A cloud
Covers the sun. It will not rain. I stand
In this noonday darkness somewhere between
A cross and a star, strip off my clothes, rags
That hide my bones. Bones. Bones fighting to bare
Their blankness to open air. I strip, listen
To the sound of my skin scrape against the earth,

And dance to the music of the only instrument
I ever learned to play: the dirt. The silent,
Too silent, biographer, the earth. The earth.

———

The Stricken
PAUL WILLIS (American, contemporary)

If light of morning has to do with you,
it has to do with anyone who wants
a new beginning. They do say it's true
a single soul in suffering still haunts
the places it once paced when in the flesh.
But souls do suffer in this dark life too,
and every dawn brings respite, yet brings fresh
regrets as well, as only dawn can do.
For by its glimmer we remain the same,
not changed in any twinkling of an eye.
We pace where we have paced—afflicted, lame,
still suffering that touch upon the thigh.
But could the sun illuminate your soul,
the dark would limp away and leave you whole.

———

What Would I Give?
CHRISTINA ROSSETTI (English, 1830–1894)

What would I give for a heart of flesh to warm me thro',
Instead of this heart of stone ice-cold whatever I do;
Hard and cold and small, of all hearts the worst of all.

What would I give for words, if only words would come;
But now in its misery my spirit has fallen dumb:
O merry friends, go your way, I have never a word to say.

What would I give for tears, not smiles but scalding tears,
To wash the black mark clean, and to thaw the frost of years,
To wash the stain ingrain and to make me clean again.

———

Psalm 55

Mary Sidney Herbert, Countess of Pembroke
 (English, 1561–1621)

My God, most glad to look, most prone to hear,
      An open ear, oh, let my prayer find,
            And from my plaint turn not thy face away.
            Behold my gestures, hearken what I say,
      While uttering moans with most tormented mind,
My body I no less torment and tear.
For, lo, their fearful threat'nings would mine ear,
      Who griefs on griefs on me still heaping lay,
            A mark to wrath and hate and wrong assigned;
            Therefore, my heart hath all his force resigned
      To trembling pants; death terrors on me pray;
I fear, nay, shake, nay, quiv'ring quake with fear.

Then say I, oh, might I but cut the wind,
      Borne on the wing the fearful dove doth bear:
            Stay would I not, till I in rest might stay.
            Far hence, oh, far, then would I take my way
      Unto the desert, and repose me there,
These storms of woe, these tempests left behind.
But swallow them, O Lord, in darkness blind,

Confound their counsels, lead their tongues astray,
That what they mean by words may not appear.
For mother Wrong within their town each where,
And daughter Strife their ensigns so display,
As if they only thither were confined.

These walk their city walls both night and day;
Oppressions, tumults, guiles of every kind
Are burgesses and dwell the middle near;
About their streets his masking robes doth wear
Mischief clothed in deceit, with treason lined,
Where only he, he only bears the sway.
But not my foe with me this prank did play,
For then I would have borne with patient cheer
An unkind part from whom I know unkind,
Nor he whose forehead Envy's mark had signed,
His trophies on my ruins sought to rear,
From whom to fly I might have made assay.

But this to thee, to thee impute I may,
My fellow, my companion, held most dear,
My soul, my other self, my inward friend:
Whom unto me, me unto whom did bind
Exchanged secrets, who together were
God's temple wont to visit, there to pray.
Oh, let a sudden death work their decay,
Who speaking fair such cankered malice mind,
Let them be buried breathing in their bier;
But purple morn, black ev'n, and midday clear
Shall see my praying voice to God inclined,
Rousing him up, and naught shall me dismay.

He ransomed me; he for my safety fined
In fight where many sought my soul to slay;

He, still himself to no succeeding heir
    Leaving his empire shall no more forbear
But at my motion, all these atheists pay,
By whom, still one, such mischiefs are designed.
Who but such caitiffs would have undermined,
    Nay, overthrown, from whom but kindness mere
        They never found? Who would such trust betray?
        What buttered words! Yet war their hearts bewray.
    Their speech more sharp than sharpest sword or spear
Yet softer flows than balm from wounded rind.

But my o'erloaden soul, thyself upcheer,
    Cast on God's shoulders what thee down doth weigh
        Long borne by thee with bearing pained and pined:
        To care for thee he shall be ever kind;
    By him the just in safety held away
Changeless shall enter, live, and leave the year:
But, Lord, how long shall these men tarry here?
    Fling them in pit of death where never shined
        The light of life, and while I make my stay
        On thee, let who their thirst with blood allay
    Have their life-holding thread so weakly twined
That it, half-spun, death may in sunder shear.

———

Tears

ELIZABETH BARRETT BROWNING (English, 1806–1861)

Thank God, bless God, all ye who suffer not
More grief than ye can weep for. That is well—
That is light grieving! lighter, none befell
Since Adam forfeited the primal lot.
Tears! what are tears? The babe weeps in its cot,

The mother singing; at her marriage-bell
The bride weeps, and before the oracle
Of high-faned hills the poet has forgot
Such moisture on his cheeks. Thank God for grace,
Ye who weep only! If, as some have done,
Ye grope tear-blinded in a desert place
And touch but tombs,—look up! those tears will run
Soon in long rivers down the lifted face,
And leave the vision clear for stars and sun.

———

FROM *The Gifts of the Christ Child*
GEORGE MACDONALD (Scottish, 1824–1905)

[Editor's Note: Phosy's story continues early on Christmas morning as she holds the tiny baby she has found lying on the bed in the spare room. Convinced he is the Baby Jesus, whom she believes is literally born each Christmas, she gradually senses that all is not well. The household stirs: her nurse Alice and her father, Mr. Greatorex, soon discover her.]

She sat for a time still as marble waiting for marble to awake, heedful as tenderest woman not to rouse him before his time, though her heart was swelling with the eager petition that he would ask his Father to be as good as chasten her. And as she sat, she began, after her wont, to model her face to the likeness of his, that she might understand his stillness—the absolute peace that dwelt on his countenance. But as she did so, again a sudden doubt invaded her: Jesus lay so very still—never moved, never opened his pale eye-lids! And now set thinking, she noted that he did not breathe. She had seen babies asleep, and their breath came and went—their little bosoms heaved up and down, and sometimes they would smile, and sometimes they would moan and sigh. But

Jesus did none of all these things: was it not strange? And then he was cold—oh, so cold!

A blue silk coverlid lay on the bed: she half rose and dragged it off, and contrived to wind it around herself and the baby. Sad at heart, very sad, but undismayed, she sat and watched him on her lap.

Meantime the morning of Christmas Day grew. The light came and filled the house. The sleepers slept late, but at length they stirred. Alice awoke last—from a troubled sleep, in which the events of the night mingled with her own lost condition and destiny. After all Polly had been kind, she thought, and got Phosy up without disturbing her.

She had been but a few minutes down, when a strange and appalling rumor made itself—I cannot say audible, but—somehow known through the house, and every one hurried up in horrible dismay.

The nurse had gone into the spare room, and missed the little dead thing she had laid there. The bed was between her and Phosy, and she never saw her. The doctor had been sharp with her about something the night before: she now took her revenge in suspicion of him, and after a hasty and fruitless visit of inquiry to the kitchen, hurried to Mr. Greatorex.

The servants crowded to the spare room, and when their master, incredulous indeed, yet shocked at the tidings brought him, hastened to the spot, he found them all in the room, gathered at the foot of the bed. A little sunlight filtered through the red window-curtains, and gave a strange pallid expression to the flame of the candle, which had now burned very low. At first he saw nothing but the group of servants, silent, motionless, with heads leaning forward, intently gazing: he had come just in time: another moment and they would have ruined the lovely sight. He stepped forward, and saw Phosy, half shrouded in blue, the candle behind illuminating the hair she had found too rebellious to the brush, and making of it a faint aureole about her head and white face, whence cold and sorrow had driven all the flush, rendering it colorless as that upon her arm which had never seen the light. She had pored on the little face until she knew death, and now she sat a speechless mother of sorrow, bending in the dim light of the tomb over the body of her holy infant.

How it was I cannot tell, but the moment her father saw her she looked up, and the spell of her dumbness broke.

"Jesus is dead," she said, slowly and sadly, but with perfect calmness. "He is dead," she repeated. "He came too early, and there was no one up to take care of him, and he's dead—dead—dead!"

But as she spoke the last words, the frozen lump of agony gave way; the well of her heart suddenly filled, swelled, overflowed; the last word was half sob, half shriek of utter despair and loss.

Alice darted forward and took the dead baby tenderly from her. The same moment her father raised the little mother and clasped her to his bosom. Her arms went round his neck, her head sank on his shoulder, and sobbing in grievous misery, yet already a little comforted, he bore her from the room.

"No, no, Phosy!" they heard him say, "Jesus is not dead, thank God. It is only your little brother that hadn't life enough, and is gone back to God for more."

EPIPHANY WEEK 5

Among the Fallen

OPENING PRAYER
I take my heart in my hand,
  O my God, O my God,
My broken heart in my hand:
  Thou hast seen, judge Thou.
My hope was written on sand,
  O my God, O my God;
Now let Thy judgment stand—
  Yea, judge me now.
—CHRISTINA ROSSETTI (English, 1830–1894)

SCRIPTURES
PSALM 102 | MICAH 7:1–7 | ROMANS 7:14–25 | JOHN 8:1–11

READINGS
"Sonnet 146" by WILLIAM SHAKESPEARE
"Christmas, 2000" by SUSANNA CHILDRESS
"Snowfall" by SARAH ARTHUR
From *Notes from Underground* by FYODOR DOSTOEVSKY

PERSONAL PRAYER AND REFLECTION

CLOSING PRAYER
The heavy weights of grief oppress me sore:
  Lord, raise me by thy word,
As thou to me didst promise heretofore.
  And this unforced praise

I for an off'ring bring, accept, O Lord,
And show to me thy ways.
—MARY SIDNEY HERBERT, COUNTESS OF PEMBROKE (English,
1561–1621)

READINGS

Sonnet 146
WILLIAM SHAKESPEARE (English, 1564–1616)

Poor soul, the center of my sinful earth,
Fooled by these rebel powers that thee array,
Why dost thou pine within and suffer dearth,
Painting thy outward walls so costly gay?
Why so large cost, having so short a lease,
Dost thou upon thy fading mansion spend?
Shall worms, inheritors of this excess,
Eat up thy charge? Is this thy body's end?
Then, soul, live thou upon thy servant's loss,
And let that pine to aggravate thy store;
Buy terms divine in selling hours of dross;
Within be fed, without be rich no more:
    So shalt thou feed on death, that feeds on men,
    And death once dead, there's no more dying then.

———

Christmas, 2000
SUSANNA CHILDRESS (American, contemporary)

My father has a pocket full of things even he does not know. In the
    morning
      with his cup, snow outside the window and his church across
        the way, the early hours have called him *man* at their first birr
        of light,
sent from the sun with a name. This Christmas, nothing is wrong: my
    brother
      has not dyed his hair, my sister passed her boards, I am not in
      love
    with a black man. This Christmas I notice how my uncles close him
      out of conversation like a musty room, effectually sending him
to the couch with Uncle Jim, who is on his way to, if not already,

drunk, and who is most interesting of them all, watching football from
    inside
    a featherless mind. My uncles say, *Alfalfa? Hayseed?* On the sides
      of his eyes, my father's skin droops into Greek letters. This is
    the year—
I should have guessed even then, in the quick clasp of holiday—my
    father
    will call forth my sympathy, small, consistent buckets carried
    in
from the shore of adolescence, where he banned me,
    where I crawled in the foam of his crashed voice, his pulling
fury. We do not, probably we will never, talk about the day

I found his hands around my throat, not squeezing—not squeezing
    at all, but holding, perhaps for the sake of what he did not know
    how to wield, perhaps in the sheer, ensconced loss of control,
his cloak of red-white-&-blue so soiled and so electrifying. Though I

do not know it yet,

this is the year I will cry for my father in a wet stratagem:
knowledge,

distance, despair. At first this is despite myself, my fear of him
unable to sour into a wholesome hate, easing instead
into an uncertainty, a loss spilling over, his own wounds

wounding me: in the caverns of his mouth they say, *I do not know*
if my father loved me; in his bones, the venom of circumstance; in
every thing,

everything, Vietnam. This is how it began, my body on the
floor,

reckless, yelling out his terrible, forgiven name to God. No—this is how
it began: there, on the couch with Jim, head thrown back, lips
slightly open, fallen asleep, his face stepped back from its sturdy
pulpit. The bad dream he is having furrows his skin, tells how
his old, rapacious core is susceptible to horror and rush,

the helplessness of a dream, the dark temper, perhaps, turned on him,
heavying his heavy pocket. My father stopped being strong.
This is the year I learn that fear runs, in fact, on legs
of love, but it will be months before I breathe a prayer to topple
its velocity. It is only Christmas, and we have gathered
in one room, the periodicity of gifts packing us tight
to each other's bodies, laughing, coughing. Families—these units of
purpose,

cannot, even when there is nothing else, learn the language of stillness.
My father is awake, picking something from his ear. I have my hands
in my pockets, the surest place for my fingers. Grandmother
and the Christmas Tree sit in opposite corners of the enlivened room,
keeping

the world so coolly in a kind of balance. Here is what we are,

here is what we wish to be: perched inside the ruby ornament, given
to the sinking
of meringue, trusting as the Towhee at the feeder each carefully pecked
winter morning.

———

Snowfall
SARAH ARTHUR (American, contemporary)

When the snow falls
it falls like death
in slow layers
and keeps falling
till nothing we have known
    is known.
We stand silent in the woods
awaiting the wide white twilight.

They say when you die of cold
you fall asleep first.
    And so I wonder:
If you die of snow
like a princess do you dream
for a hundred years
while a blanket of white
mounds over your chest
and pines stand silent
in the trackless deep
and not even the mice
know you're there?
If a tree falls in the snow
does it sleep for a hundred years?

And if you prick your finger
and a drop of red blood
falls on the silent snow
do the woods shudder
with strange violence;
does the snow rot
with dark undergrowth;
do the dead leaves bleed?
Does the woodsman then awake,
shoulder his ax, slay his brother in the field?

O, wash me with hyssop
    and I shall be clean;
Wash me with snow
    and I shall be whiter than I was.

Lay me down in a drift
that I may slip off to sleep
and do not wake me till spring
when the woodsman comes
to lay his ax
    at the root of the trees.

———

FROM *Notes from Underground*
FYODOR DOSTOEVSKY (Russian, 1821–1881)

[Editor's Note: Dostoevsky mastered the art of creating despicable characters with whom the reader can empathize. In this disturbing novella the narrator—himself miserable and cut off from humanity—describes an unpremeditated attempt to be a better man than he really is by promising to rescue the prostitute Liza from her dead-end life. The next morning, when she embarrasses him by visiting his apartment, he shatters her hopes by treating her like a charity case.]

G ood-bye," she said, going towards the door.
    I ran up to her, seized her hand, opened it, thrust something in it and closed it again. Then I turned at once and dashed away in haste to the other corner of the room to avoid seeing, anyway. . . .

I did intend just now to tell a lie—to write that I did this accidentally, not knowing what I was doing through foolishness, through losing my head. But I don't want to lie, and so I will say straight out that I opened her hand and put the money in it . . . from spite. It came into my head to do this while I was running up and down the room and she was sitting behind the screen. But this I can say for certain: though I did that cruel thing purposely, it was not an impulse from the heart, but came from my evil brain. This cruelty was so affected, so purposely made up, so completely a product of the brain, of books, that I could not even keep it up a minute—first I dashed away to avoid seeing her, and then in shame and despair rushed after Liza. I opened the door in the passage and began listening.

"Liza! Liza!" I cried on the stairs, but in a low voice, not boldly. There was no answer, but I fancied I heard her footsteps, lower down on the stairs.

"Liza!" I cried, more loudly.

No answer. But at that minute I heard the stiff outer glass door open heavily with a creak and slam violently; the sound echoed up the stairs.

She had gone. I went back to my room in hesitation. I felt horribly oppressed.

I stood still at the table, beside the chair on which she had sat and looked aimlessly before me. A minute passed, suddenly I started; straight before me on the table I saw. . . . In short, I saw a crumpled blue five-rouble note, the one I had thrust into her hand a minute before. It was the same note; it could be no other, there was no other in the flat. So she had managed to fling it from her hand on the table at the moment when I had dashed into the further corner.

Well! I might have expected that she would do that. Might I have expected it? No, I was such an egoist, I was so lacking in respect for my fellow-creatures that I could not even imagine she would do so. I could not endure it. A minute later I flew like a madman to dress, flinging on what I could at random and ran headlong after her. She could not have got two hundred paces away when I ran out into the street.

It was a still night and the snow was coming down in masses and falling almost perpendicularly, covering the pavement and the empty street as though with a pillow. There was no one in the street, no sound was to be heard. The street lamps gave a disconsolate and useless glimmer. I ran two hundred paces to the cross-roads and stopped short.

Where had she gone? And why was I running after her?

Why? To fall down before her, to sob with remorse, to kiss her feet, to entreat her forgiveness! I longed for that, my whole breast was being rent to pieces, and never, never shall I recall that minute with indifference. But—what for? I thought. Should I not begin to hate her, perhaps, even tomorrow, just because I had kissed her feet today? Should I give her happiness? Had I not recognized that day, for the hundredth time, what I was worth? Should I not torture her?

I stood in the snow, gazing into the troubled darkness and pondered this.

"And will it not be better?" I mused fantastically, afterwards at home, stifling the living pang of my heart with fantastic dreams. "Will it not be better that she should keep the resentment of the insult for ever? Resentment—why, it is purification; it is a most stinging and painful consciousness! Tomorrow I should have defiled her soul and have exhausted her heart, while now the feeling of insult will never die in her heart, and however loathsome the filth awaiting her—the feeling of insult will elevate and purify her . . . by hatred . . . h'm! . . . perhaps, too, by forgiveness. . . . Will all that make things easier for her though? . . ."

And, indeed, I will ask on my own account here, an idle question: which is better—cheap happiness or exalted sufferings? Well, which is better?

So I dreamed as I sat at home that evening, almost dead with the pain in my soul. Never had I endured such suffering and remorse, yet could there have been the faintest doubt when I ran out from my lodging that I should turn back half-way? I never met Liza again and I have heard nothing of her. I will add, too, that I remained for a long time afterwards pleased with the phrase about the benefit from resentment and hatred in spite of the fact that I almost fell ill from misery.

Even now, so many years later, all this is somehow a very evil memory. I have many evil memories now, but . . . hadn't I better end my "Notes" here? I believe I made a mistake in beginning to write them, anyway I have felt ashamed all the time I've been writing this story; so it's hardly literature so much as a corrective punishment. Why, to tell long stories, showing how I have spoiled my life through morally rotting in my corner, through lack of fitting environment, through divorce from real life, and rankling spite in my underground world, would certainly not be interesting; a novel needs a hero, and all the traits for an anti-hero are *expressly* gathered together here, and what matters most, it all produces an unpleasant impression, for we are all divorced from life, we are all cripples, every one of us, more or less. We are so divorced from it that we feel at once a sort of loathing for real life, and so cannot bear to be reminded of it. Why, we have come almost to looking upon real life as an effort, almost as hard work, and we are all privately agreed that it is better in books. And why do we fuss and fume sometimes? Why are we perverse and ask for something else? We don't know what ourselves. It would be the worse for us if our petulant prayers were answered. Come, try, give any one of us, for instance, a little more independence, untie our hands, widen the spheres of our activity, relax the control and we . . .

yes, I assure you . . . we should be begging to be under control again at once. I know that you will very likely be angry with me for that, and will begin shouting and stamping. Speak for yourself, you will say, and for your miseries in your underground holes, and don't dare to say all of us—excuse me, gentlemen, I am not justifying myself with that "all of us." As for what concerns me in particular I have only in my life carried to an extreme what you have not dared to carry halfway, and what's more, you have taken your cowardice for good sense, and have found comfort in deceiving yourselves. So that perhaps, after all, there is more life in me than in you. Look into it more carefully! Why, we don't even know what living means now, what it is, and what it is called? Leave us alone without books and we shall be lost and in confusion at once. We shall not know what to join on to, what to cling to, what to love and what to hate, what to respect and what to despise. We are oppressed at being men—men with a real individual body and blood, we are ashamed of it, we think it a disgrace and try to contrive to be some sort of impossible generalized man. We are stillborn, and for generations past have been begotten, not by living fathers, and that suits us better and better. We are developing a taste for it. Soon we shall contrive to be born somehow from an idea. But enough; I don't want to write more from "Underground."

EPIPHANY WEEK 6

Love's Offices

OPENING PRAYER

Drop Thy still dews of quietness
Till all our strivings cease;
Take from our souls the strain and stress,
And let our ordered lives confess
The beauty of Thy peace.
—JOHN GREENLEAF WHITTIER (American, 1807–1892)

SCRIPTURES

PSALM 134 | ISAIAH 53:7–12 | HEBREWS 11:32–40 |
LUKE 20:45–47, 21:1–4

READINGS

"Those Winter Sundays" by ROBERT HAYDEN
"Those Who Carry" by ANNA KAMIEŃSKA
"Work and Contemplation" by ELIZABETH BARRETT BROWNING
"Matins" by GEORGE HERBERT
"Whatsoever is right, that shall ye receive" by CHRISTINA ROSSETTI
From *The Snow Queen* by HANS CHRISTIAN ANDERSEN

PERSONAL PRAYER AND REFLECTION

CLOSING PRAYER

Lord, thou hast carried me through this evening's duty;
I am released, weary, and well content.
O soul, put on the evening dress of beauty,
Thy sunset-flush, of gold and purple blent!
Alas, the moment I turn to my heart,

Feeling runs out of doors, or stands apart,
But such as I am, Lord, take me as thou art.
—George MacDonald (Scottish, 1824–1905)

READINGS

Those Winter Sundays
Robert Hayden (African-American, 1913–1980)

Sundays too my father got up early
and put his clothes on in the blueblack cold,
then with cracked hands that ached
from labor in the weekday weather made
banked fires blaze. No one ever thanked him.

I'd wake and hear the cold splintering, breaking.
When the rooms were warm, he'd call,
and slowly I would rise and dress,
fearing the chronic angers of that house,

Speaking indifferently to him,
who had driven out the cold
and polished my good shoes as well.
What did I know, what did I know
of love's austere and lonely offices?

———

Those Who Carry
Anna Kamieńska (Polish, 1920–1986)

Those who carry grand pianos
to the tenth floor wardrobes and coffins

the old man with a bundle of wood hobbling toward the horizon
the lady with a hump of nettles
the madwoman pushing her baby carriage
full of empty vodka bottles
they all will be raised up
like a seagull's feather like a dry leaf
like an eggshell a scrap of newspaper on the street

Blessed are those who carry
for they will be raised

———

Work and Contemplation
ELIZABETH BARRETT BROWNING (English, 1806–1861)

The woman singeth at her spinning-wheel
A pleasant chant, ballad or barcarole;
She thinketh of her song, upon the whole,
Far more than of her flax; and yet the reel
Is full, and artfully her fingers feel
With quick adjustment, provident control,
The lines—too subtly twisted to unroll—
Out to a perfect thread. I hence appeal
To the dear Christian Church—that we may do
Our Father's business in these temples mirk,
Thus swift and steadfast, thus intent and strong;
While thus, apart from toil, our souls pursue
Some high calm spheric tune, and prove our work
The better for the sweetness of our song.

———

Matins
GEORGE HERBERT (English, 1593–1633)

I cannot ope mine eyes,
But thou art ready there to catch
My morning-soul and sacrifice:
Then we must needs for that day make a match.

My God, what is a heart?
Silver, or gold, or precious stone,
Or star, or rainbow, or a part
Of all these things, or all of them in one?

My God, what is a heart?
That thou shouldst it so eye, and woo,
Pouring upon it all thy art,
As if that thou hadst nothing else to do?

Indeed man's whole estate
Amounts (and richly) to serve thee:
He did not heav'n and earth create,
Yet studies them, not him by whom they be.

Teach me thy love to know;
That this new light, which now I see,
May both the work and workman show:
Then by a sunbeam I will climb to thee.

———

"Whatsoever is right, that shall ye receive."
CHRISTINA ROSSETTI (English, 1830–1894)

When all the overwork of life
Is finished once, and fallen asleep
We shrink no more beneath the knife,

But having sown prepare to reap;
Delivered from the crossway rough,
   Delivered from the thorny scourge,
   Delivered from the tossing surge,
Then shall we find—(please God!)—it is enough?

Not in this world of hope deferred,
   This world of perishable stuff;
Eye hath not seen, nor ear hath heard,
   Nor heart conceived that full "enough":
Here moans the separating sea,
   Here harvests fail, here breaks the heart;
   There God shall join and no man part,
All one in Christ, so one—(please God!)—with me.

———

FROM *The Snow Queen*
HANS CHRISTIAN ANDERSEN (Danish, 1805–1875)

[Editor's note: In a tale that may have provided inspiration for some of C. S. Lewis's **The Lion, the Witch, and the Wardrobe**, shards of glass from a broken magic mirror become lodged in the eye and heart of the boy Kay, eventually distorting his character. This leads him to fall for the wiles of the Snow Queen, who makes him prisoner in her frozen northern palace. His loving and loyal friend Gerda goes on an adventure to save him, aided by various creatures. We join her on the last leg of the journey.]

Oh! I have not got my boots! I have not brought my gloves!" cried little Gerda. She remarked she was without them from the cutting frost; but the Reindeer dared not stand still; on he ran till he came to the great bush with the red berries, and there he set Gerda down, kissed her mouth, while large bright tears flowed from the animal's eyes, and then back he went as fast as possible. There stood poor Gerda now, without shoes or gloves, in the very middle of dreadful icy Finland.

She ran on as fast as she could. There then came a whole regiment of snow-flakes, but they did not fall from above, and they were quite bright and shining from the Aurora Borealis. The flakes ran along the ground, and the nearer they came the larger they grew. Gerda well remembered how large and strange the snow-flakes appeared when she once saw them through a magnifying-glass; but now they were large and terrific in another manner—they were all alive. They were the outposts of the Snow Queen. They had the most wondrous shapes; some looked like large ugly porcupines; others like snakes knotted together, with their heads sticking out; and others, again, like small fat bears, with the hair standing on end: all were of dazzling whiteness—all were living snow-flakes.

Little Gerda repeated the Lord's Prayer. The cold was so intense that she could see her own breath, which came like smoke out of her mouth. It grew thicker and thicker, and took the form of little angels, that grew more and more when they touched the earth. All had helms on their heads, and lances and shields in their hands; they increased in numbers; and when Gerda had finished the Lord's Prayer, she was surrounded by a whole legion. They thrust at the horrid snow-flakes with their spears, so that they flew into a thousand pieces; and little Gerda walked on bravely and in security. The angels patted her hands and feet; and then she felt the cold less, and went on quickly towards the palace of the Snow Queen.

But now we shall see how Kay fared. He never thought of Gerda, and least of all that she was standing before the palace.

The walls of the palace were of driving snow, and the windows and doors of cutting winds. There were more than a hundred halls there, according as the snow was driven by the winds. The largest was many miles in extent; all were lighted up by the powerful Aurora Borealis, and all were so large, so empty, so icy cold, and so resplendent! Mirth never reigned there; there was never even a little bear-ball, with the storm for music, while the polar bears went on their hind legs and showed off their steps. Never a little tea-party of white young lady foxes; vast, cold, and empty were the halls of the Snow Queen. The northern-lights shone with such precision that one could tell exactly when they were at their highest or lowest degree of brightness. In the middle of the empty, endless hall of snow, was a frozen lake; it was cracked in a thousand pieces, but each piece was so like the other, that it seemed the work of a cunning artificer. In the middle of this lake sat the Snow Queen when she was at home; and then she said she was sitting in the Mirror of Understanding, and that this was the only one and the best thing in the world.

Little Kay was quite blue, yes, nearly black with cold; but he did not observe it, for she had kissed away all feeling of cold from his body, and his heart was a lump of ice. He was dragging along some pointed flat pieces of ice, which he laid together in all possible ways, for he wanted to make something with them; just as we have little flat pieces of wood to make geometrical figures with, called the Chinese Puzzle. Kay made all sorts of figures, the most complicated, for it was an ice-puzzle for the understanding. In his eyes the figures were extraordinarily beautiful, and of the utmost importance; for the bit of glass which was in his eye caused this. He found whole figures which represented a written word; but he never could manage to represent just the word he wanted—that word was "eternity"; and the Snow Queen had said, "If you can discover that figure, you shall be your own master, and I will make you a present of the whole world and a pair of new skates." But he could not find it out.

"I am going now to the warm lands," said the Snow Queen. "I must have a look down into the black caldrons." It was the volcanoes Vesuvius and Etna that she meant. "I will just give them a coating of white, for that is as it ought to be; besides, it is good for the oranges and the grapes." And then away she flew, and Kay sat quite alone in the empty halls of ice that were miles long, and looked at the blocks of ice, and thought and thought till his skull was almost cracked. There he sat quite benumbed and motionless; one would have imagined he was frozen to death.

Suddenly little Gerda stepped through the great portal into the palace. The gate was formed of cutting winds; but Gerda repeated her evening prayer, and the winds were laid as though they slept; and the little maiden entered the vast, empty, cold halls. There she beheld Kay: she recognized him, flew to embrace him, and cried out, her arms firmly holding him the while, "Kay, sweet little Kay! Have I then found you at last?"

But he sat quite still, benumbed and cold. Then little Gerda shed burning tears; and they fell on his bosom, they penetrated to his heart, they thawed the lumps of ice, and consumed the splinters of the looking-glass; he looked at her, and she sang the hymn:

"The rose in the valley is blooming so sweet; And angels descend there the children to greet."

Hereupon Kay burst into tears; he wept so much that the splinter rolled out of his eye, and he recognized her, and shouted, "Gerda, sweet little Gerda! Where have you been so long? And where have I been?" He looked round him. "How cold it is here!" said he. "How empty and cold!" And he held fast by Gerda, who laughed and wept for joy. It was so beautiful, that even the blocks of ice danced about for joy; and when they were tired and laid themselves down, they formed exactly the letters which the Snow Queen had told him to find out; so now he was his own master, and he would have the whole world and a pair of new skates into the bargain.

Gerda kissed his cheeks, and they grew quite blooming; she kissed his eyes, and they shone like her own; she kissed his hands and feet, and he was again well and merry. The Snow Queen might come back as soon as she liked; there stood his discharge written in resplendent masses of ice.

EPIPHANY WEEK 7

Turning Back

OPENING PRAYER

Lord Jesus, think on me,
And purge away my sin;
From earthborn passions set me free,
And make me pure within.
—Adapted from the poetry of SYNESIUS (Greek, AD 375–430)

SCRIPTURES

PSALM 6 | ISAIAH 55:6–13 | 2 CORINTHIANS 5:16–20 |
LUKE 17:11–19

READINGS

"Classicism" by ANNA KAMIEŃSKA
"The Search" by GEORGE HERBERT
"St. Agnes' Eve" by ALFRED, LORD TENNYSON
"Non-Disparagement Agreement" by MARY F. C. PRATT
From *Mr. Ives' Christmas* by OSCAR HIJUELOS

PERSONAL PRAYER AND REFLECTION

CLOSING PRAYER

Ah my dear angry Lord
Since Thou dost love, yet strike;
Cast down, yet help afford;
Sure I will do the like.

I will complain, yet praise;
I will bewail, approve:

And all my sour-sweet days
I will lament, and love.
—GEORGE HERBERT (English, 1593–1633)

READINGS

Classicism
ANNA KAMIEŃSKA (Polish, 1920–1986)

The weather is so foul
it would be good to read Marcus Aurelius
to call forth the light of pure thought
The intellect when it really tries
can for a time replace the sun
though it won't ripen strawberries

It promenades in cloisters
pearly sky between columns
air steaming round plum trees in bloom

One thing not even thought can do
is to forgive
in particular to forgive the living
their pain despair and life

———

The Search
GEORGE HERBERT (English, 1593–1633)

Whither, O, whither art Thou fled,
            My Lord, my Love?

My searches are my daily bread;
                Yet never prove.

My knees pierce th' earth, mine eyes the sky;
                And yet the sphere
And centre both to me deny
                That Thou art there.

Yet can I mark how herbs below
                Grow green and gay,
As if to meet Thee they did know,
                While I decay.

Yet can I mark how stars above
                Simper and shine,
As having keys unto Thy love,
                While poor I pine.

I sent a sigh to seek Thee out,
                Deep drawn in pain,
Wing'd like an arrow: but my scout
                Returns in vain.

I turned another (having store)
                Into a groan;
Because the search was dumb before:
                But all was one.

Lord, dost Thou some new fabric mould
                Which favor wins,
And keeps thee present, leaving th' old
                Unto their sins?

Where is my God? what hidden place
                Conceals Thee still?
What covert dare eclipse Thy face?
                Is it Thy will?

O let not that of anything;
                    Let rather brass,
Or steel, or mountains be Thy ring,
                    And I will pass.

Thy will such an entrenching is,
                    As passeth thought:
To it all strength, all subtleties
                    Are things of nought.

Thy will such a strange distance is,
                    As that to it
East and West touch, the poles do kiss,
                    And parallels meet.

Since then my grief must be as large,
                    As is Thy space,
Thy distance from me; see my charge,
                    Lord, see my case.

O take these bars, these lengths away;
                    Turn, and restore me:
Be not Almighty, let me say,
                    Against, but for me.

When Thou dost turn, and wilt be near;
                    What edge so keen,
What point so piercing can appear
                    To come between?

For as Thy absence doth excel
                    All distance known:
So doth Thy nearness bear the bell,
                    Making two one.

St. Agnes' Eve

ALFRED, LORD TENNYSON (English, 1809–1892)

Deep on the convent-roof the snows
    Are sparkling to the moon:
My breath to heaven like vapor goes:
    May my soul follow soon!
The shadows of the convent-towers
    Slant down the snowy sward,
Still creeping with the creeping hours
    That lead me to my Lord:
Make Thou my spirit pure and clear
    As are the frosty skies,
Or this first snowdrop of the year
    That in my bosom lies.

As these white robes are soil'd and dark,
    To yonder shining ground;
As this pale taper's earthly spark,
    To yonder argent round;
So shows my soul before the Lamb,
    My spirit before Thee;
So in mine earthly house I am,
    To that I hope to be.
Break up the heavens, O Lord! and far,
    Thro' all yon starlight keen,
Draw me, thy bride, a glittering star,
    In raiment white and clean.

He lifts me to the golden doors;
    The flashes come and go;
All heaven bursts her starry floors,
    And strows her lights below,
And deepens on and up! the gates

Roll back, and far within
For me the Heavenly Bridegroom waits,
    To make me pure of sin.
The sabbaths of Eternity,
    One Sabbath deep and wide—
A light upon the shining sea—
    The Bridegroom with his bride!

———

Non-Disparagement Agreement
MARY F. C. PRATT (American, contemporary)

After David Weinstock

If you won't tell how I cried,
I won't tell how you left.
You won't tell my raging, either,
how I blamed you for everything:
my sister's dying, the terrorists,
war, cancer and pain, blindness,
stupidity.
So you won't tell
how I slammed doors, broke goblets,
made a fool of myself every time
I remembered. And I won't tell how
quiet you were, how you wouldn't
turn back when I called.
I won't tell
of the blank, the emptiness
of the faceless winter sky
with its perfect stillness of stars,
the hollowness of the laughter
at feasts, the blandness of Rilke

and Bach.
You mocked me
with happinesses, with sunrises
and hymns, but I won't tell.
You won't tell how I tried,
and later, how I stopped trying,
believing as fervently in your absence,
and I won't tell
how it amazes me
that people still fall in love,
that somebody in that shabby
brown house practices Beethoven's
piano sonatas with all the windows open,
that strangers dig through the rubble
with bare hands, over and over,
trying to pull strangers back to life.
And especially I won't tell
how you returned,
how the stories went on,
how the grass grew
green again and again after the snows,
the days lengthened, the chicks hatched
and the moon rose in a thin
white shard.

———

FROM *Mr. Ives' Christmas*

OSCAR HIJUELOS (Cuban-American, 1951–2013)

[Editor's note: After many years Mr. Ives finds himself agreeing to meet with Daniel Gomez—the man who, as a teenager, had killed Mr. Ives' son. Gomez has served his time and is now married with stepsons.]

Gomez's house was not like some of the splendid houses one would see driving around Troy; it was close to the train station, and although it was set on a lot between two higher buildings, in which mainly working-class families lived, the street itself was rundown, the very steps to his front door in need of repair. Ives and Ramirez parked, and upon approaching the entranceway saw Father Jimenez, an old man now in wire-rim glasses peering out from behind the screen. Ives was nervous. Something was strangling inside, and he worried that it might be some kind of coronary. He carried in one hand a box of bakery cookies, which he had bought because he remembered that the couple had two kids, and an envelope. Ramirez followed him and was carrying a small night bag, which he kept on his lap during the hour or so that they were there, fidgeting restlessly during the "meeting."

Ives wore a tie and jacket, and when he was led in, he thought that whether they owned a restaurant or not these people were poor. Ives was startled. It was almost a repetition of the apartment he remembered visiting on 137th Street years before: the furniture was either worn or cheaply new and covered with plastic. The color television was the biggest and newest piece of furniture. There was shelving with little bric-a-brac here and there, cheap throw rugs, family photographs in Woolworth's frames, and a crucifix and plaster Virgin Mary with Child on a table; the kitchen was small and narrow, with a backdoor that led out to a porch where garbage cans and bicycles were piled.

Her two sons, twelve and fourteen, were out working, but there was evidence that they had just been there. There were plates on a card table covered with leftover food and a half-empty bottle of soda. In the corner of the living room stood an artificial blue-green tree.

Gomez himself had been putting on a jacket in the bathroom, when his wife called up the stairs, shouting, "Dan, they're here."

He had been so nervous about finally meeting with Ives that he had spent half the morning throwing up and trying to relieve himself on the toilet. No sooner had he looked out the window, seeing Ives and Ramirez pulling up, that his attacks started all over again. Pushing open the door, he shouted, "Be down in a minute," then spent another few minutes trying to collect himself. He was tremendously heavy, about three hundred pounds now, his head sweaty, his walk lumbering: although he had to live with the two tear-shaped tattoos on his face and still retained an air of severity, his expression, as he came down the stairs, was that of a penitent. He had put on a blue suit, a tie. His scuffed black shoes had been brightened with some enamel paint.

But when he stood on the landing and first saw Mr. Ives, he was somehow relieved: he had expected a face of torment or wrath or unending sorrow and had found an older white-haired man in a tie and jacket, almost demurely standing with his hat in hand, head lowered, his face filled with compassion. And for his part Ives, who had spent the morning replaying his son's death over and over in his head, had expected the hardened convict of an earlier photograph. Now there he was: Ives found himself trembling—with rage, joy, forgiveness? And was his stomach in knots because he felt like leaping forward and strangling the man?

But he controlled himself and, like a fine gentleman, his smile restrained, he strode forward and put his arms around Gomez, who had started to cry, over the very goodness he had glimpsed so briefly just then in Ives' gaze. Gomez awkwardly reciprocated, and he was touched by the scent of cologne about the face of a man who had quite carefully shaved that morning, his skin, in those moments, releasing so much pent-up grief and forgiveness, sweet as church incense. And Gomez found himself repeating, "Thank you for coming here, sir. Thank you, and God bless you."

In those moments, Ives knew, his son was somewhere in that room, and approving of what he beheld.

The Second Advent

OPENING PRAYER

Teach me to live, that I may dread
The grave as little as my bed;
Teach me to die, that so I may
Rise glorious at the awful day.
—THOMAS KEN (English, 1637–1711)

SCRIPTURES

PSALM 2 | MALACHI 3:1–5 | REVELATION 11:15–19 |
MATTHEW 24:29–44

READINGS

". . . for who can endure the day of his coming?" by LUCI SHAW
From "In Memoriam A. H. H." by ALFRED, LORD TENNYSON
"The End of Heaven and the End of Hell" by SCOTT CAIRNS
From "On the Morning of Christ's Nativity: The Hymn" by JOHN MILTON
"Later Life: A Double Sonnet of Sonnets (I)" by CHRISTINA ROSSETTI
"Judgment Day" by MARY F. C. PRATT
"The Coming of the King" by LAURA E. RICHARDS

PERSONAL PRAYER AND REFLECTION

CLOSING PRAYER

In supplication meek
To Thee I bend the knee;
O Christ, when Thou shalt come,
In love remember me,

And in Thy kingdom, by Thy grace,
Grant me a humble servant's place.

—Adapted from the poetry of GREGORY OF NAZIANZUS
(Cappadocia/modern-day Turkey, AD 325–390)

READINGS

". . . for who can endure the day of his coming?"
LUCI SHAW (naturalized U.S. citizen, contemporary)

Malachi 3:2

When an angel
snapped the old thin threads of speech
with an untimely birth announcement,
slit the seemly cloth of an even more blessed
event with shears of miracle,
invaded the privacy of a dream, multiplied
to ravage the dark silk of the sky,
the innocent ears, with swords of sound:
news in a new dimension demanded
qualification. The righteous were
as vulnerable as others. They trembled
for those strong antecedent *Fear nots*,
whether goatherds, virgins, workers
in wood, or holy barren priests.

In our nights
our complicated modern dreams
rarely flower into visions. No contemporary
Gabriel dumbfounds our worship,

or burning, visits our bedrooms.
No signpost satellite hauls us, earthbound
but star-struck, half around the world
with hope. Are our sensibilities too blunt
to be assaulted with spatial power-plays
and far-out proclamations of peace?
Sterile, skeptics, yet we may be broken
to his slow, silent birth, his beginning
new in us. His big-ness may still burst
our self-containment to tell us,
without angels' mouths, *Fear not.*

God knows we need to hear it, now,
when he may shatter, with his most shocking
coming, this proud, cracked place,
and more if, for longer waiting,
he does not.

————

FROM *"In Memoriam A. H. H."*
ALFRED, LORD TENNYSON (English, 1809–1892)

O yet we must trust that somehow good
    Will be the final goal of ill,
    To pangs of nature, sins of will,
Defects of doubt, and taints of blood;

That nothing walks with aimless feet;
    That not one life shall be destroy'd,
    Or cast as rubbish to the void,
When God hath made the pile complete;

That not a worm is cloven in vain;
    That not a moth with vain desire

Is shrivell'd in a fruitless fire,
Or but subserves another's gain.

Behold, we know not anything;
  I can but trust that good shall fall
    At last—far off—at last, to all,
And every winter change to spring.

So runs my dream; but what am I?
  An infant crying in the night;
  An infant crying for the light;
And with no language but a cry.

———

"The End of Heaven and the End of Hell" FROM
the poem cycle *Disciplinary Treatises*
SCOTT CAIRNS (American, contemporary)

At long last the feeble fretwork tumbles
apart forever and you stand alone,
unprotected, undeceived, in fullness.
And we are all there as well, equally

alone and equally full of . . . Ourselves.
Yes, I believe Ourselves is what we then
become, though what *that* is must surprise
each trembling figure; and in horror

or elation the effect will be the same
humility, one of two discrete sorts,
perhaps, but genuine humility.
And that long record of our choices—your

every choice—is itself the final
body, the eternal dress. And, of course,

there extends before us finally a measure
we can recognize. We see His Face

and see ourselves, and flee. And shame—old
familiar—will sustain that flight unchecked,
or the Ghost, forgotten just now—merest
spark at the center—will flare, bid us turn

and flame unto a last consuming light:
His light, our light, caught at last together
as a single brilliance, extravagant,
compounding awful glories as we burn.

———

FROM *"On the Morning of Christ's Nativity: The Hymn"*
JOHN MILTON (English, 1608–1674)

XIII

. . . Ring out, ye crystal spheres!
Once bless our human ears,
    (If ye have power to touch our senses so;)
And let your silver chime
Move in melodious time;
    And let the bass of heaven's deep organ blow;
And with your ninefold harmony
Make up full consort of the angelic symphony.

XIV

For, if such holy song
Enwrap our fancy long,
    Time will run back and fetch the Age of Gold;
And speckled Vanity
Will sicken soon and die,

And leprous Sin will melt from earthly mould;
And Hell itself will pass away,
And leave her dolorous mansions of the peering day.

XV

Yes, Truth and Justice then
Will down return to men,
   The enameled arras of the rainbow wearing;
And Mercy set between,
Throned in celestial sheen,
   With radiant feet the tissued clouds down steering;
And Heaven, as at some festival,
Will open wide the gates of her high palace-hall.

XVI

But wisest Fate says No,
This must not yet be so;
   The Babe lies yet in smiling infancy
That on the bitter cross
Must redeem our loss,
   So both himself and us to glorify:
Yet first, to those chained in sleep,
The wakeful trump of doom must thunder through the deep,

XVII

With such a horrid clang
As on Mount Sinai rang,
   While the red fire and smoldering clouds outbrake:
The aged Earth, aghast
With terror of that blast,
   Shall from the surface to the centre shake,
When, at the world's last sessiön,
The dreadful Judge in middle air shall spread his throne.

XVIII

And then at last our bliss
Full and perfect is,
  But now begins; for from this happy day
The Old Dragon under ground,
In straiter limits bound,
  Not half so far casts his usurpèd sway,
And, wroth to see his Kingdom fail,
Swindges the scaly horror of his folded tail . . .

XXVI

. . . So, when the Sun in bed,
Curtained with cloudy red,
  Pillows his chin upon an orient wave,
The flocking shadows pale
Troop to the infernal jail,
  Each fettered ghost slips to his several grave,
And the yellow-skirted Fays[11]
Fly after the night-steeds, leaving their moon-loved maze.

XXVII

But see! the Virgin blest
Hath laid her Babe to rest,
  Time is our tedious song should here have ending:
Heaven's youngest-teemèd star
Hath fixed her polished car,
  Her sleeping Lord with handmaid lamp attending;
And all about the courtly stable
Bright-harnessed Angels sit in order serviceable.

———

Later Life: A Double Sonnet of Sonnets (I)
CHRISTINA ROSSETTI (English, 1830–1894)

Before the mountains were brought forth, before
   Earth and the world were made, then God was God:
And God will still be God, when flames shall roar
   Round earth and heaven dissolving at His nod:
   And this God is our God, even while His rod
Of righteous wrath falls on us smiting sore:
And this God is our God for evermore
   Thro' life, thro' death, while clod returns to clod.
For tho' He slay us we will trust in Him;
   We will flock home to Him by divers ways:
   Yea, tho' He slay us we will vaunt His praise,
Serving and loving with the Cherubim,
Watching and loving with the Seraphim,
   Our very selves His praise thro' endless days.

———

Judgment Day
MARY F. C. PRATT (American, contemporary)

When the angel with the flaming sword asks:
What have you done that is good?
What have you done that will last?
This is the answer I will give:
I walked long with my husband
on wild uphill footpaths
remembering the names of flowers.
I gave thanks on a cold blue morning
while the new-raised sun
spread my shadow
along the unmarked snow.

I kept rosemary in a white pot
in my kitchen window.
I held my sister's hand ten days before she died
and we watched the sky turn orange one more time
and listened to a meadowlark
and did not need to speak.
I played the piano for an old man in a nursing-home:
"when the roll is called up yonder," and he sang.
I counted shooting-stars with my son
one summer midnight
and felt the skin of dew-covered grass
pulling us in safe.
The day before a February storm,
I took in a thin silver stray cat
with eyes the color of green olives.
I sat most of an afternoon in the sun
with my old dog, and later we rolled in leaves.
I trust that these will suffice.

———

The Coming of the King
LAURA E. RICHARDS (American, 1850–1943)

Some children were at play in their playground one day, when a messenger rode through the town, blowing a trumpet, and crying aloud, "The King! The King passes by this road today. Make ready for the King!"

The children stopped their play and looked at one another.

"Did you hear that?" they said. "The King is coming. He may look over the wall and see our playground; who knows? We must put it in order."

The playground was sadly dirty. In the corners were scraps of paper and broken toys, for these were careless children. But now, one brought a hoe, and another a rake, and a third ran to get the wheelbarrow from behind the garden gate. They worked hard, until finally all was clean and tidy.

"Now it is clean!" they said. "But we must make it pretty, too, for kings are used to fine things. Maybe he would not notice just cleanness, for he may have it all the time."

Then one brought sweet rushes and spread them on the ground. Others made garlands of oak leaves and pine tassels and hung them on the walls. The littlest one pulled marigold buds and threw them all about the playground, "to look like gold," he said.

When all was done the playground was so beautiful that the children stood and looked at it, and clapped their hands with pleasure.

"Let us keep it always like this!" said the littlest one. And the others cried, "Yes! Yes! That is what we will do."

They waited all day for the coming of the King, but he never came. Toward sunset, a man with travel-worn clothes and a kind, tired face passed along the road. He stopped to look over the wall.

"What a pleasant place!" said the man. "May I come in and rest, dear children?"

The children brought him in gladly. They set him on the seat that they had made out of an old barrel. They had covered it with an old red cape to make it look like a throne, and it made a very good one.

"It is our playground!" they said. "We made it pretty for the King, but he did not come, and now we mean to keep it so for ourselves."

"That is good!" said the man.

"Because we think pretty and clean is nicer than ugly and dirty!" said another.

"That is better!" said the man.

"And for tired people to rest in!" said the littlest one.

"That is best of all!" said the man.

He sat and rested, and looked at the children with such kind eyes that they came around him. They told him all they knew—about the five puppies in the barn, and the bird's nest with four blue eggs, and the shore where the gold shells grew. The man nodded and understood all about it.

By and by he asked for a cup of water, and they brought it to him in the best cup, with the gold sprigs on it. Then he thanked the children, and rose and went on his way. But before he went he laid his hand on their heads for a moment, and the touch went warm to their hearts.

The children stood by the wall and watched the man as he went slowly along. The sun was setting, and the light fell in long slanting rays across the road.

"He looks so tired!" said one of the children.

"But he was so kind!" said another. "See!" said the littlest one. "How the sun still shines on his hair! It looks like a crown of gold."

FINAL WEEK IN EPIPHANY

Light Upon Light

OPENING PRAYER

O Light that knew no dawn,
That shines to endless day,
All things in earth and heaven
Are lustered by Thy ray;
No eye can to Thy throne ascend,
Nor mind Thy brightness comprehend.
—Adapted from the poetry of GREGORY OF NAZIANZUS
(Cappadocia/modern-day Turkey, AD 325–390)

SCRIPTURES

PSALM 148 | ISAIAH 60:1–9 | 1 JOHN 1:5–10 | MATTHEW 5:13–16

READINGS

"A Psalm at the Sunrise" by WALTER WANGERIN JR.
"In the Father's Glory Shining" by SYNESIUS
"Canticle of the Sun" by ST. FRANCIS OF ASSISI
"Quiet Time" by ELIZABETH B. ROONEY
"Compline" by DICK ALLEN
From *The Pilgrim's Progress: Part II* by JOHN BUNYAN

PERSONAL PRAYER AND REFLECTION

CLOSING PRAYER

Thy grace, O Father, give,
That I may serve in fear;
Above all boons, I pray,

Grant me Thy voice to hear;
From sin Thy child in mercy free,
And let me dwell in light with Thee.
—Adapted from the poetry of GREGORY OF NAZIANZUS
(Cappadocia/modern-day Turkey, AD 325–390)

READINGS

A Psalm at the Sunrise
WALTER WANGERIN JR. (American, contemporary)

Omnipotens sempiterne Deus![12]
Almighty God, the Everlasting, Thou! I cannot look steadfastly at
the sun and not go blind. Holiness exceeds my sight—though I
know it is, as I know thou art.

Aeterne Deus omnium rerum Creator!
Thou art above all created things. To everything made, thou art the
Other. Greater than thee there is no world; in thee all worlds have
being; and I take my trivial, mortal way upon the smallest sphere of
all. How shall I hope to see thee and not die?

Lux Mundi!
But in thy mercy thou shinest down upon the things that thou hast
made. They brighten in thy light. Every morning they reflect thee. I
wake to an effulgence of mirrors, and lo: I see.

Misericors Deus!
For my sake, for my poor fleshly sight, thou changest thy terrible
holiness here before me into glory—the visible light, the doxology I
can see. I rise and look around, and I cry praise to thee.

Deus, incommutabilis virtus, lumen aeternum!

From thee to me it is a mighty diminution: ever the same, thou makest thy presence manifest in things that are both mutable and common. But from me to thee it is epiphany: gazing at things most common, suddenly I see thy light, thy glory, and thy face.

Nobiscum Deus!

Then what shall I say to thee but Deo Gratias? Thanks be to God.

Deo gratias!

For the dew that damps the morning grasses is a baptism, always, always renewing the earth. And the air remembers that once it ushered down the dove that was the breath of God. And I myself inhale the rinsed spirit of the morning air and am renewed.

Deo gratias!

For dawn, in the chalices of the clouds, brims them with a bloody wine, a running crimson. And this is a sign to me. The sun is coming.

Deo gratias!

For the sun, when it breaks at the horizon, transfigures everything. And this is a gift to me. For the transfiguration itself persuades my soul of sunrise.

Jesu filio Dei gratias!

For I have seen a baby sleeping in a shaft of sunlight, and behold: in the curve of every eyelash was a small sun cupped. From these fringes, tiny rays shot forth to sting me. Sunrise at the far horizon was sunrise near me in this infant.

Et verbum caro factum est—

For the baby suddenly opened her mouth and yawned. And into that pink cavern rushed the sunlight, trembling and flashing like a living thing. But it was thee, bright God, in the mouth of a mortal infant.

"Ecce ego vobiscum sum—"

For the baby woke to the morning and saw me close beside her, and she smiled. Ah, God! What an epiphany of smiling that was! My own transfiguration! For this was the primal light, the glory of the morning, thy splendor and thy face before me come.

Deo gratias, cuius gloria!
Then glory be to thee, Father, Son, and Holy Spirit, as it was in the beginning, is now, and ever shall be, *in saecula saeculorum.*

Amen.

————

In the Father's Glory Shining
SYNESIUS (Greek, AD 375–430)

In the Father's glory shining
Jesus, Light of light art Thou;
Sordid night before Thee fleeth,—
On our souls Thou'rt falling now.

Framer of the world, we hail Thee!
Thou didst mould the stars of night;
Earth to life Thou dost awaken,
Savior Thou, of glorious might!

'Tis Thy hand that guides the chariot
When the sun illumes the skies,
And the dark of night relaxes
When Thou bidst the moon arise.

At Thy word the harvest ripens,
Flocks and herds their pasture find;
Earth gives bread to feed the hungry,
For the hand of God is kind.

May my soul, her want perceiving,
Turn her gaze to where Thou art,
And in all Thy fullness find Thee
Food to satisfy the heart.

Canticle of the Sun
St. Francis of Assisi (Italian, ca. 1181–1226)

Most high, all powerful, all good Lord!
All praise is yours, all glory, all honor, and all blessing.
To you, alone, Most High, do they belong.
No mortal lips are worthy to pronounce your name.
Be praised, my Lord, through all your creatures,
especially through my lord Brother Sun,
who brings the day; and you give light through him.
And he is beautiful and radiant in all his splendor!
Of you, Most High, he bears the likeness.
Be praised, my Lord, through Sister Moon and the stars;
in the heavens you have made them bright, precious and beautiful.
Be praised, my Lord, through Brothers Wind and Air,
and clouds and storms, and all the weather,
through which you give your creatures sustenance.
Be praised, My Lord, through Sister Water;
she is very useful, and humble, and precious, and pure.
Be praised, my Lord, through Brother Fire,
through whom you brighten the night.
He is beautiful and cheerful, and powerful and strong.
Be praised, my Lord, through our sister Mother Earth,
who feeds us and rules us,
and produces various fruits with colored flowers and herbs.
Be praised, my Lord, through those who forgive for love of you;
through those who endure sickness and trial.
Happy those who endure in peace,
for by you, Most High, they will be crowned.
Be praised, my Lord, through our Sister Bodily Death,
from whose embrace no living person can escape.
Woe to those who die in mortal sin!
Happy those she finds doing your most holy will.

The second death can do no harm to them.
Praise and bless my Lord, and give thanks,
and serve him with great humility.

———

Quiet Time
Elizabeth B. Rooney (American, 1924–1999)

Now are we winter deep
In quietness.
The shadowed snow,
The gliding owl,
The moon
Keep silent vigil now.

We can be still,
So still we start to know
The depth of everything,
So still we hear the stars
Begin to sing.

———

"Compline" from the poem cycle *The Canonical Hours*
Dick Allen (American, contemporary)

For those who can't reach back, be Thou their gift.
But for ourselves, Lord, for ourselves we ask
Light mercies, also. Show us truer tasks
Than those yet known to us. Although night drifts
Across our portion of the planet, you will lift
The darkness up again, and we shall bask

In sunlight when it ends—your cold death mask
Broken by re-dawning of belief.

We are as children now, who ask you guide
Us safely into sleep, and lead us through
The valley to still waters, pasture land
Green with the tall grass where brown spiders hide.
When hope seems ended, let us be with you,
Risen at this most ungodly hour, God.

———

FROM *The Pilgrim's Progress: Part II*
JOHN BUNYAN (English, 1628–1688)

[Editor's note: Part I of **The Pilgrim's Progress** traces the journey of
Christian, who leaves his wife and family in search of the Celestial
City. Part II tells the story of his wife, Christiana, and their children,
who repent and follow the path Christian took. Eventually they, too,
arrive on the shore of the river over which they must cross to reach
their destination. It is a land of grace and light, where Christiana pre-
pares to meet the King.]

After this, I beheld until they were come unto the Land of
Beulah, where the sun shineth night and day. Here, because
they were weary, they betook themselves awhile to rest. And because
this country was common for pilgrims, and because the orchards
and vineyards that were here belong to the King of the Celestial
Country, therefore they were permitted to make bold with any of
His things. But a little while soon refreshed them here; for the bells
did so ring, and the trumpets continually sound so melodiously,
that they could not sleep and yet they received as much refreshing
as if they had slept their sleep never so soundly. Here also the noise
of them that walked in the streets was, "More pilgrims are come
to town!" And another would answer, saying, "And so many went

over the water, and were let in at the golden gates, to-day!" They would cry again, "There is now a legion of Shining Ones just come to town, by which we know that there are more pilgrims upon the road; for here they come to wait for them, and comfort them after all their sorrow!" Then the pilgrims got up, and walked to and fro. But how were their ears now filled with heavenly voices, and their eyes delighted with celestial visions! In this land they heard nothing, saw nothing, felt nothing, smelt nothing, tasted nothing, that was offensive to their stomach or mind; only when they tasted of the water of the river over which they were to go, they thought that it tasted a little bitterish to the palate, but it proved sweeter when it was down.

In this place there was a record kept of the names of them that had been pilgrims of old, and a history of all the famous acts that they had done. It was here also much spoken of, how the river to some had had its flowings, and what ebbings it had had while others have gone over. It has been in a manner dry for some, while it has overflowed its banks for others.

In this place, the children of the town would go into the King's gardens, and gather nosegays for the pilgrims, and bring them to them with much affection. Here also grew camphire, with spikenard, and saffron, calamus, and cinnamon, with all the trees of frankincense, myrrh, and aloes, with all chief spices. With these the pilgrims' chambers were perfumed while they stayed here; and with these were their bodies anointed, to prepare them to go over the river, when the time appointed was come.

Now, while they lay here, and waited for the good hour, there was a noise in the town that there was a messenger come from the Celestial City with matter of great importance to one Christiana, the wife of Christian the pilgrim. So inquiry was made for her, and the house was found out where she was. So the messenger presented her with a letter; the contents whereof were, "Hail, good woman! I bring thee tidings that the Master calleth for thee, and expecteth that thou shouldest stand in His presence, in clothes of everlasting life, within these ten days."

When he had read this letter to her, he gave her therewith a sure token that he was a true messenger, and was come to bid her make haste to be gone. The token was an arrow, with a point sharpened with love, let easily into her heart, which by degrees wrought so effectually with her, that at the time appointed she must be gone.

When Christiana saw that her time was come, and that she was the first of this company that was to go over, she called for Mr. Great-heart, her guide, and told him how matters were. So he told her he was heartily glad of the news, and could have been glad had the post come for him. Then she bid that he should give advice how all things should be prepared for her journey. So he told her, saying, "Thus and thus it must be; and we that are left will accompany you to the river-side."

Then she called for her children, and gave them her blessing, and told them that she yet read with comfort the mark that was set in their foreheads, and was glad to see them with her there, and that they had kept their garments so white. Lastly, she gave to the poor that little she had, and commanded her sons and her daughters to be ready against the messenger should come for them. . . .

. . . Now, the day drew on that Christiana must be gone. So the road was full of people to see her take her journey. But, behold, all the banks beyond the river were full of horses and chariots, which were come down from above to accompany her to the City gate. So she came forth and entered the river, with a beckon of farewell to those that followed her to the river-side. The last words that she was heard to say were, "I come, Lord, to be with Thee, and bless Thee!"

CLOSING THOUGHTS

As our readings draw to a close, we have made the turn toward the light, climbing up and out of the year's root cellar. The longest night has come and gone. By the end of Epiphany we have caught a glimpse of the next season ahead, the early hints of spring and the promise of new life and resurrection. But with Lent comes a hallowed awareness that the road may grow harder before the final and everlasting joy. Our Savior will exchange his crown of glory for one of thorns. Yet the promise of Christmas is that the light will not be quenched: darkness does not have the last word. May you take the light from these readings into the next season of the journey.

FOR FURTHER READING

Many of the following works were read or consulted during the creation of this anthology. Though not an exhaustive list, it offers a jumping-off point for deeper exploration of the themes prevalent during Advent, Christmas, and Epiphany.

Fiction
- *Silas Marner* by George Eliot, particularly chapter 10 of book one
- "The Little Match Girl" by Hans Christian Andersen
- *Even Unto Bethlehem* by Henry van Dyke
- *Wind in the Willows* by Kenneth Grahame
- "The Gift of the Magi" by O. Henry
- *The Last Battle* by C. S. Lewis
- *Maria Chapdelaine* by Louis Hémon
- *The Give-Away* and *The Christmas Moccasins* by Ray Buckley
- *The Abundance: A Novel* by Amit Majmudar
- *Saint Maybe* by Anne Tyler

Poetry
- "Paradise Regained" by John Milton
- *The Tragedy of Hamlet, Prince of Denmark* by William Shakespeare
- "Christmas Bells" by Henry Wadsworth Longfellow
- "The Magi" and "The Second Coming" by William Butler Yeats
- "Carol of the Brown King" and the play "Black Nativity" by Langston Hughes
- "Journey of the Magi" and "A Song for Simeon" by T. S. Eliot, from *The Complete Poems and Plays: 1909–1950*

- "Star of the Nativity" and "December 24, 1971" by Joseph Brodsky, from *Collected Poems in English*
- "Christmas Eve" and "Annunciation" from the collection *A Pentecost of Finches* by Robert Siegel
- "A Death in Advent" and "Mysteries of the Incarnation: She Said Yeah" by Kathleen Norris from *Little Girls in Church*
- *Renaming Ecstasy: Latino Writings on the Sacred* edited by Orlando Ricardo Menes
- "And the Angel Left Her" by Angela Alaimo O'Donnell, from *Saint Sinatra and Other Poems*
- *The Flag of Childhood: Poems from the Middle East* selected by Naomi Shihab Nye
- "Psalm: First Forgive the Silence" by Mark Jarman, anthologized in *Bearing the Mystery: Twenty Years of IMAGE*, edited by Gregory Wolfe
- *A Widening Light: Poems of the Incarnation* edited by Luci Shaw
- "Christmas Eve 1945," "New York, Christmas Eve, 1947," "Mantra for a Dark December Night," and "The Fathers" by Paul Mariani, from *Epitaphs for the Journey*
- *Imago Dei: Poems from Christianity and Literature* by Jill Peláez Baumgaertner

ACKNOWLEDGMENTS AND PERMISSIONS

There are many, many people to thank for making this book possible, not the least of which are the various caregivers for my two small boys: Krista Zielinski Fuerst, Alice McKinstry, Tabitha Martin, Katie Soltis, Gretchen Williams, and Shelley Mull. To all the grandparents, especially Bob and Peg Faulman, who consider helping me with the boys a ministry to my readers. And above all to my very busy pastor-husband, Tom, who potty-trained our toddler and took on many extra household tasks in order for this book to happen. It is an honor to share life, faith, and ministry with you.

Acknowledgment is gratefully made for permission to include the following works or excerpts:

ALLEN, DICK: "Compline" first published in *Image: A Journal of Arts and Religion* and in the anthology *Bearing the Mystery: Twenty Years of IMAGE* (William B. Eerdmans Publishing Company, 2009) edited by Gregory Wolfe; "Solace" first published in *This Shadowy Place: Poems* (St. Augustine's Press, 2014). Used by permission of the author.

ARTHUR, SARAH: "Advent in Michigan" first published in the journal *Time of Singing* (Winter 2002) and in *The One Year Coffee With God* (Tyndale House Publishers, 2007). Used by permission.

BIELOUSOVA, GRAŽINA: "Childhood Stories" first published in *Lógia* 3 (April 2006), a publication of the Divinity School at Duke University. Used by permission of the author.

BUECHNER, FREDERICK: excerpt from *Godric* (HarperOne, an imprint of HarperCollins Publishers). Copyright 1980 by Frederick Buechner. Used by permission of Frederick Buechner Literary Assets, LLC.

CAIRNS, SCOTT: selected poems from *Compass of Affection: Poems New and Selected.* Copyright 2006 by Scott Cairns. Used by permission of Paraclete Press: www.paracletepress.com.

CHILDRESS, SUSANNA: "Bethlehem, Indiana" first published in *Perspectives* (December 2010); "Christmas, 2000" first published in *Black Creek Review* (Summer 2002). Used by permission of the author.

HAYDEN, ROBERT: "Those Winter Sundays" from *Collected Poems of Robert Hayden*, edited by Frederick Glaysher. Copyright 1966 by Robert Hayden. Used by permission of Liveright Publishing Corporation.

HIJUELOS, OSCAR: "Not Enough Wine or Scotch" and excerpt from "In Troy," from *Mr. Ives' Christmas.* Copyright 1995 by Oscar Hijuelos. Reprinted by permission of HarperCollins Publishers.

IRVING, JOHN: excerpt from *A Prayer for Owen Meany.* Copyright 1989 by Garp Enterprises, Ltd. Reprinted by permission of HarperCollins Publishers.

JOHNSON, MARCI RAE: "Conversion" first published in *Relief*; "O That With Yonder Sacred Throng" first published in *Rock & Sling.* Used by permission of the author.

KAMIEŃSKA, ANNA: selected poems from *Astonishments: Selected Poems of Anna Kamieńska.* Copyright 2007 by Paweł Śpiewak. Translation and compilation copyright 2007 by Grażyna Drabik and David Curzon. Used by permission of Paraclete Press: www.paracletepress.com.

LEE, LI-YOUNG: "Nativity" and "The Eternal Son" from *Book of My Nights.* Copyright 2001 by Li-Young Lee. Reprinted with the permission of The Permissions Company, Inc., on behalf of BOA Editions, Ltd., www.boaeditions.org.

MAJMUDAR, AMIT: "Seventeens: Incarnation" from *Heaven and Earth* (Story Line Press, 2011). Used by permission of the author.

MARIANI, PAUL: "Shadow of the Father" from *Deaths and Transfigurations*. Copyright 2005 by Paul Mariani. Use by permission of Paraclete Press: www.paracletepress.com.

MILLS, JOAN RAE: "Mary" used by permission of the author.

OKORO, ENUMA: "Advent" used by permission of the author.

PETERSON, EUGENE: "Day VI: The War" published in *Once Upon a Christmas: A Treasury of Memories*, compiled and edited by Emilie Griffin (The C. R. Gibson Company, 1993). Used by permission of the author.

PRATT, MARY F. C.: "Writing a Sermon, December 23" first published in *The Other Side* (Winter 1999); and "Judgment Day" in *The Witness* (December 1998). These and other selected poems used by permission of the author.

RHODES, SUZANNE UNDERWOOD: "Advent" first published in *What a Light Thing, This Stone* (Sow's Ear Press, 1999). Used by permission of the author.

ROONEY, ELIZABETH B.: selected poems from *Gift Wrapped*, the fourth volume in her collected works *All Miracle* (Brigham Farm Publishing, 2001). Used by permission of the Elizabeth B. Rooney Family Trust. www.brighamfarm.com.

RUNYAN, TANIA: "Mary at the Nativity" first published in the journal *Willow Springs* and in *Delicious Air* (Finishing Line Press, 2007), *Simple Weight* (FutureCycle Press, 2010), and *A Thousand Vessels* (WordFarm, 2011); "Shepherd at the Nativity" and "Joseph at the Nativity" first appeared in *Simple Weight*. Used by permission of the author.

SÁENZ, BENJAMÍN ALIRE: "Cemetery" first published in *Calendar of Dust* (Broken Moon Press, 1991); "The Adoration of the Infant Jesus" first published in *Dark and Perfect Angels* (Cinco Puntos Press, 1996). Used by permission of the author.

SCHMIDT, GARY D.: excerpt from *The Wednesday Wars*. Copyright 2009 by Gary D. Schmidt. Reprinted by permission of Clarion Books, an imprint of Houghton Mifflin Harcourt Publishing Company. All rights reserved.

SHAW, LUCI: ". . . for who can endure the day of his coming?" and "Made Flesh" from *Accompanied by Angels: Poems of the Incarnation* (William B. Eerdmans Publishing Company, 2006); and "It is as if infancy were the whole of incarnation" from *Polishing the Petoskey Stone: New and Selected Poems* (Harold Shaw Publishers, 1990). Used by permission of the author.

WALKER, JEANNE MURRAY: "Flight" first published in *The Cresset*; "Staying Power" first published in *Poetry*. Used by permission of the author.

WALSH, CHAD: "A quintina of crosses" from *A Widening Light: Poems of the Incarnation*, edited by Luci Shaw (Harold Shaw Publishers, 1984). Used by permission.

WANGERIN, WALTER, JR.: "The Christmas Story" and "A Psalm at the Sunrise" published in *Once Upon a Christmas: A Treasury of Memories*, compiled and edited by Emilie Griffin (The C. R. Gibson Company, 1993). Used by permission of the author.

WILLIS, PAUL: "Christmas Child" first published in *The Lamp-Post* (1997) and *Say This Prayer into the Past* (Cascade Books, 2014); "The Forest Primeval" first published in *Kinesis* (1997) and *Visiting Home* (Pecan Grove Press, 2008); "Freeman Creek Grove" first published in *Sierra Heritage* (1991) and *Visiting*

Home; "The Stricken" first published in *Windhover* (2012). Used by permission of the author.

CONTRIBUTORS

DICK ALLEN, the Connecticut State Poet Laureate from 2010–2015, is the author of nine books of poetry, including the 2013 New Criterion Prize-winning *This Shadowy Place* (St. Augustine's; Fall 2014). http://home.earthlink.net/~rallen285/

GRAŽINA BIELOUSOVA is an English and biblical studies instructor at LCC International University and the Evangelical Bible Institute in Lithuania. A graduate of Duke University Divinity School in Durham, North Carolina, she is a regular contributor to various evangelical magazines, an incurable daydreamer, a voracious reader, and an aspiring gardener.

FREDERICK BUECHNER is a writer-theologian and the author of over thirty books ranging from novels to autobiography and sermons. A finalist for both the National Book Award and the Pulitzer, he has won many awards and been recognized by the American Academy and Institute of Arts and Letters. www.frederickbuechner.com

SCOTT CAIRNS is an author, poet, and memoirist whose works have been highly anthologized. A recipient of a Guggenheim Fellowship in 2006, he serves on the faculty of the University of Missouri.

SUSANNA CHILDRESS is the author of two award-winning books of poetry, *Jagged with Love* (University of Wisconsin Press, 2005) and *Entering the House of Awe* (New Issues Press, 2011). She writes fiction and creative nonfiction and, with musician Joshua Banner, comprises the band Ordinary Neighbors. www.susannachildress. com

JOHN IRVING is the internationally acclaimed author of thirteen novels and has won numerous awards, including an Oscar for his screenplay adaptation of *The Cider House Rules*.

MARCI RAE JOHNSON teaches English at Valparaiso University, where she serves as Poetry Editor for *The Cresset*. She is also the poetry editor for WordFarm press. Her first collection of poetry won the Powder Horn Prize and will be published by Sage Hill Press. http://marciraejohnson.blogspot.com/

LI-YOUNG LEE is an award-winning poet and autobiographer. His poetry collection *Book of My Nights* won the William Carlos Williams award in 2002.

AMIT MAJMUDAR is a novelist, poet, essayist, and diagnostic nuclear radiologist. His poetry collection *Heaven and Earth* was awarded the Donald Justice Prize for 2011. www.amitmajmudar.com

PAUL MARIANI is an award-winning poet, essayist, biographer, and university professor of English at Boston College.

JOAN RAE MILLS teaches English as a Second Language at Delaware Technical and Community College in Georgetown, Delaware. Her work has been published in anthologies, the NIV Women's Devotional Bible, and over fifty different magazines.

ENUMA OKORO is a writer, speaker, and spiritual director whose books include *Reluctant Pilgrim* (Fresh Air Books, 2010) and *Silence and Other Surprising Invitations of Advent* (Upper Room Books, 2012). www.enumaokoro.com

EUGENE PETERSON is a pastor, poet, author, and scholar best known for *The Message* paraphrase of the Bible in contemporary language, for which he won the Gold Medallion Book Award.

MARY F. C. PRATT was born in Vermont and hasn't come up with a good enough reason to leave. She is a (mostly) retired deacon in the Episcopal Church. http://gladerrand.wordpress.com

SUZANNE UNDERWOOD RHODES is an award-winning poet whose books include *What a Light Thing, This Stone* and *Weather of the*

House (both from Sow's Ear Press), and two volumes of prose poems/ meditations: *A Welcome Shore* and *Sketches of Home* (Canon Press). http://rhodesnottaken.com/

TANIA RUNYAN is the author of the collections *Second Sky*, *A Thousand Vessels*, *Simple Weight*, and *Delicious Air*, which won Book of the Year by the Conference on Christianity and Literature. She is also an NEA fellow, editor, private tutor, and very busy mom.

BENJAMÍN ALIRE SÁENZ is a poet, novelist, artist, and writer of children's books. His latest collection of short stories was the winner of the 2013 Pen Faulkner Award for Fiction; he is the first Hispanic to ever win that award. He teaches in the bilingual creative writing department at the University of Texas at El Paso.

GARY D. SCHMIDT is a National Book Award finalist and professor of English at Calvin College. The author of numerous nonfiction books and young adult novels, he received both a Newbery Honor and a Printz Honor for *Lizzie Bright and the Buckminster Boy* and a Newbery Honor for *The Wednesday Wars*.

LUCI SHAW is a lifelong poet, author, editor, speaker, retreat facilitator, and, since 1988, writer in residence at Regent College in Vancouver, Canada. Author of over thirty books, she has most recently published *Scape* (Wipf and Stock, 2013) and the nonfiction prose reflection *Adventure of Ascent: Field Notes from a Lifelong Journey* (IVP, 2014). www.lucishaw.com

JEANNE MURRAY WALKER serves as a professor of English at the University of Delaware and as a mentor in Seattle Pacific University's Masters of Fine Arts Program. Her books include *New Tracks*, *Night Falling*, *Geography of Memory*, and *New and Selected Poems*. www.jeannemurraywalker.com

WALTER WANGERIN JR. is the author of more than thirty books for all ages, including *The Book of the Dun Cow*, which won the National

Book Award. He holds the Jochum Chair at Valparaiso University in Valparaiso, Indiana, where he teaches literature and creative writing, and is writer-in-residence. http://walterwangerinjr.org

PAUL J. WILLIS is a professor of English at Westmont College and a former poet laureate of Santa Barbara, California. His most recent book of poems is *Say This Prayer into the Past* (Poiema Poetry, 2014). www.pauljwillis.com

NOTES

1. See the entry on "Epiphany" in *The New Westminster Dictionary of Liturgy and Worship*, edited by Paul Bradshaw (Louisville, KY: Westminster John Knox Press, 2002). Why this particular date in January, scholars are uncertain: perhaps it had to do with calculations related to Easter.

2. Ibid; see the entry on "Christmas."

3. The second season of Ordinary Time runs from Pentecost Sunday in the spring to the last Saturday before Advent. It is the longest season of the church year.

4. Translated by John Mason Neale (English, 1818–1866).

5. A monogram for the name of Jesus Christ, originally from the Greek.

6. Translated by William Wordsworth (English, 1770–1850).

7. "Swain" is a country youth, or shepherd; "Solyma" is an ancient name for Jerusalem.

8. Spinks and ouzels are types of birds.

9. "The light will shine today. . . ."

10. "Brother" in Spanish.

11. Another word for fairy, or supernatural creature.

12. *Omnipotens sempiterne Deus!* (Almighty, everlasting God!)
    Aeterne Deus omnium rerum Creator! (Eternal God, Creator of all!)
    Lux Mundi! (Light of the world!)
    Misericors Deus! (Merciful God!)
    Deus, incommutabilis virtus, lumen aerternum! (0 God of unchangeable power, the light of eternity!)
    Nobiscum Deus! (God with us!)

Deo gratias! (Thanks be to God!)
Jesu filio Dei gratias! (Jesus, the Son of God, thanks!)
Et verbum caro factum est— (And the Word was made flesh—)
"Ecce ego vobiscum sum—" ("Behold, I am with you—")
Deo gratias, cuius gloria! (Thanks be to God, all glory!)
in saecula saeculorum (world without end)

INDEX OF AUTHORS AND SOURCES

INDEX OF SCRIPTURES

ABOUT PARACLETE PRESS

Who We Are

Paraclete Press is a publisher of books, recordings, and DVDs on Christian spirituality. Our publishing represents a full expression of Christian belief and practice—from Catholic to Evangelical, from Protestant to Orthodox.

We are the publishing arm of the Community of Jesus, an ecumenical monastic community in the Benedictine tradition. As such, we are uniquely positioned in the marketplace without connection to a large corporation and with informal relationships to many branches and denominations of faith.

What We Are Doing

PARACLETE PRESS BOOKS

Paraclete publishes books that show the richness and depth of what it means to be Christian. Although Benedictine spirituality is at the heart of all that we do, we publish books that reflect the Christian experience across many cultures, time periods, and houses of worship. We publish books that nourish the vibrant life of the church and its people.

We have several different series, including the best-selling Paraclete Essentials and Paraclete Giants series of classic texts in contemporary English; Voices from the Monastery—men and women monastics writing about living a spiritual life today; award-winning poetry; best-selling gift books for children on the occasions of baptism and first communion; and the Active Prayer Series that brings creativity and liveliness to any life of prayer.

MOUNT TABOR BOOKS

Paraclete's newest series, Mount Tabor Books, focuses on liturgical worship, art and art history, ecumenism, and the first millennium church; and was created in conjunction with the Mount Tabor Ecumenical Centre for Art and Spirituality in Barga, Italy.

Paraclete Recordings

From Gregorian chant to contemporary American choral works, our recordings celebrate the best of sacred choral music composed through the centuries that create a space for heaven and earth to intersect. Paraclete Recordings is the record label representing the internationally acclaimed choir Gloriæ Dei Cantores, praised for their "rapt and fathomless spiritual intensity" by *American Record Guide*; the Gloriæ Dei Cantores Schola, specializing in the study and performance of Gregorian chant; and the other instrumental artists of the Gloriæ Dei Artes Foundation.

Paraclete Press is also privileged to be the exclusive North American distributor of the recordings of the Monastic Choir of St. Peter's Abbey in Solesmes, France, long considered to be a leading authority on Gregorian chant.

Paraclete Video

Our DVDs offer spiritual help, healing, and biblical guidance for a broad range of life issues including grief and loss, marriage, forgiveness, facing death, bullying, addictions, Alzheimer's, and spiritual formation.

Learn more about us at our website:
www.paracletepress.com or phone us
toll-free at 1-800-451-5006

SCAN TO READ MORE

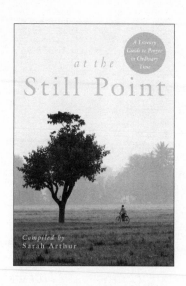

At the Still Point
A Literary Guide to Prayer in Ordinary Time
SARAH ARTHUR

"What a delight to find so extraordinary a collection meant for use in ordinary time! Any book that includes passages from *The Wind in the Willows* and *Moby Dick*, as well as poems by George Herbert and Christina Rossetti, is all right with me. . . . Each of the works chosen is meant to awaken me to the movement of the spirit in daily life."
—Kathleen Norris, author of *Dakota* and *Cloister Walk*

ISBN: 1-978-1-61261-785-7 | 280 pages | $16.99, Trade paperback

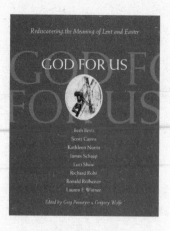

God for Us

Rediscovering the Meaning of Lent and Easter

EDITED BY GREG PENNOYER

CONTRIBUTORS INCLUDE

RICHARD ROHR, LAUREN F. WINNER, AND KATHLEEN NORRIS

ISBN: 978-1-61261-379-6 | 220 pages | $29.99

God for Us explores Lent's importance in spiritual formation, its significance in the preparation for Easter, and the holy season of Easter itself. With reflections from leading spiritual writers, histories of the liturgical calendar and feast days of the holy season, and fine art that spans over 1500 years.

Available from most booksellers or through Paraclete Press:
www.paracletepress.com
1-800-451-5006
Try your local bookstore first.